Bognor Regis
Short Story Co1

THE WEST SUS!

Meet the Winners

EDITED BY JULIA MACFARLANE

Zoom Internet was delighted to sponsor the Bognor Write Club's
first short story competition.

Congratulations to all those well-deserved winners whose work
appears in this anthology.

zoom-internet.co.uk

Aldwick Publishing Ltd

ISBN 978-1-9164024-6-1

Meet The Winners edited and produced by Julia Macfarlane of
Aldwick Publishing on behalf of the Bognor Regis Write Club
www.aldwickpublishing.com; www.bognorwriteclub.com

Cover image © Heather Robbins 2019,
based on the original poster designed by Lizzy Shephard

Table of Contents

Foreword

Imagine your favourite relative – or friend – has just given you a luxurious box of chocolates. As you lift the lid you see before you a delicious selection of unknown shapes and flavours. You can tell that each one has been crafted with skill and created with passion.

Here is your literary box of chocolates. You may not recognise all their names but you are about to settle down to experience a decadent few hours of pleasure. Some have surprisingly nutty centres, a few are sweet concoctions that will melt into your heart – and a few will, hopefully, tickle your taste buds. There is gentle humour and laugh-out-loud fun; some twists in the tale and others that will linger in your mind long after the book is finished.

When the Bognor Regis Write Cub first had the idea of launching a short story competition for our third anthology, we did not really know what to expect. We have been overwhelmed by the quality of the stories received and our team of ten judges worked diligently to choose their favourites. Each story within these pages was in at least one of our judges' top five. The final judging session was as tense as anything experienced by Costa or Booker panels, I am sure. All stories were judged anonymously. Once the winners were agreed upon and the authors' names revealed, we were humbled by the professional writers who have chosen to grace our book with their work.

The competition and the book have taken over my life for the last few months. I hope you, the reader, think it was worth it as you indulge in this cornucopia of well-written stories by our finalists.

Julia Macfarlane
Chair, Bognor Regis Write Club

Acknowledgements

The Bognor Regis Write Club would like to thank the following people and organisations for their help with the competition and the book. We couldn't have done it without you!

- Zoom Internet Ltd for their generous sponsorship
- Lizzy Shephard for designing our competition, invitation and winners' certificates
- Heather Robbins for our cover design and book preparation
- To our judges:
  - Becky Brooke
  - Anne Caine
  - Jenny Dean
  - Cosmo Goldsmith
  - Maralyn Green
  - Julia Macfarlane (www.macfarlanejuliawriter.com)
  - Jackie Thomsett
  - Caroline Travis
  - Robert Winter (robertwinterwriting.wordpress.com)
  - And one other who prefers not to be mentioned but we are truly grateful for the time and effort given.

AND THE WINNER IS ...

The Cabinet

BY LUCY FLANNERY

Our well-deserved winner has credits in theatre, radio, TV and film, in addition to fiction. Her sitcoms *Rent* and *Any Other Business* regularly get repeated on Radio 4 Extra. Her play, *Poisoned Beds* (co-written with Greg Mosse), which charts the rise and fall of Emsworth's doomed oyster industry, has been performed along the south coast. She teaches the 'Get Playwriting!' and 'Script Lab' courses at Chichester Festival Theatre and is an RLF Consultant Fellow. Her short stories 'Calm Down, Dear' and 'Tea' won the Brighton Prize and came third in the Dorset Fiction Prize, respectively.

Her comic novel *Wedding Stakes* was a finalist in the Exeter Novel Prize. She has been involved in two ACE-supported literary ventures – *Writing Edward,* for which she wrote the short story 'Sorry' about artist Edward King, and *You, Me & Everyone*, for which she produced micro-fiction and poetry which was projected onto the façade of Portsmouth Guildhall over two evenings. Lucy was the creator and founding director of Havant Literary Festival and she continues to advocate passionately for the transforming power of the arts. You can follow her on Twitter @writerflanners.

The Cabinet

BY LUCY FLANNERY

It wasn't just a piece of furniture. It was a principle, a symbol, a line in the sand. It said that my feelings matter, my needs are valid, I deserve to be listened to. It was a reminder that, although the balance of power may have shifted, I'm still a force to be reckoned with in this relationship.

I wanted somewhere to put my LPs. Somewhere better than the unlovely 1970s vinyl storage case where they currently resided, sideways, under the bed in the guest room. They were the tiny residue of my former collection, the cream of the crop. When it became obvious – obvious to me, I mean – that CDs weren't a passing phase I had reluctantly, painfully, allowed myself to be talked into a cull. Four hundred plus albums whittled down to less than fifty. These were the ones that I couldn't possibly part with, too precious in monetary or emotional terms to let go.

The Rise and Fall of Ziggy Stardust and the Spiders from Mars. Along with the rest of the nation, I had thrilled at that *Top of the Pops* appearance and felt the opening-up of barely imagined possibilities. Even my Dad's outraged expostulations about 'that woofter' could not take the edge off the exhilaration that coursed through my fifteen-year-old body.

An original copy of *The Velvet Underground and Nico* with the peelable banana sticker. Bought second-hand at a record fair aeons ago from a moron who didn't know what a prize he held. *The Songs of Leonard Cohen*: the first present Michael ever bought me. I played it incessantly after we broke up. Still get a lump when I hear 'Hey, That's No Way to Say Goodbye', even though it was me that ended it. *Abbey Road*, always my favourite Beatles album, and *Sergeant Pepper*'s there too, of course. Kate Bush – *The Hounds of Love*. 'Running Up That Hill' was playing when I met Daniel, in Tower Records. *Automatic for the People*, REM – a band I don't even like all that much but 'Everybody Hurts' was playing seven years later when he died in hospital, his shrivelled hand in mine.

These records, the songs they contain within their finely etched grooves, are part of me, part of the fabric of my life. And not just the songs: the covers, the artwork, the arcane texts on the reverse – they're part of who I am, they're in my DNA. Such treasures deserve a better home than the dusty underside of a bed in a spare room. They should be on show, an acknowledged feature of my personal history. The trouble is, they are bulky, cumbersome, uncompromising in their heft. And there's no room for them in the living room. According to Dominic.

Dominic is artistic. No, he really is. He's brilliant. He makes a living out of design. When we first got together, he was smitten enough not to laugh outright at my taste for the eccentric, my weakness for kitsch. But over the years, he's eradicated all those elements that I found quirky and fun: the 'Souvenir from Bridlington' trivet, the Action Man dangling from a trip-wire over the short flight of stairs to the roof garden, the framed print of a sign saying 'No Photocopying after 4.45' – all gone. But in their stead he has created an elegant, chic and, at the same time, astonishingly warm and welcoming interior that flows seamlessly from area to area, blurring soft greys and creams and that wonderful muted colour that isn't quite green and isn't quite blue but makes you feel as if you're in a cloud hovering above a sacred mountain or under water in some northern, mystic cave. The whole flat is glorious and exquisite and has been featured in a Sunday supplement (the photos didn't do it justice). I love every square inch and wouldn't change a thing – but I still want my records where I can see them.

"A cabinet?" Dominic pulled a face.

"It's not like it's a hideous orange pine job. It's a nice piece – beautiful wood, look. Carving's good quality but not over-elaborate. Barley twist legs. Useful shelf underneath. You could display something on there. You always like putting something unexpected in a room."

"It's a sideboard."

"Is it hell as like."

There was a subtext to this conversation, of course. I didn't actually come out and say, "It is my flat after all," but the words were there, hovering in the air between us.

"It won't fit."

"It will, I've measured." This was not exactly a lie but not exactly true either. The dimensions were given in metric. I'm firmly old money. But it can't not fit – that space is nearly eight foot wide.

"It won't go with anything."

"We could always paint it."

Dominic closed his eyes, in pain.

"I want my LPs out from under the bed. I want to be able to take them out and flip through them. I want to see them, touch them, sniff them."

"You can do that now."

"Not without risking a hernia! It's not much to ask, is it? It's not as if I'm saying I'm going to be *playing* them."

"There's nowhere to put a record player!"

"I could put it on top of the cabinet. Joke," I added, as his expression changed.

"How much is it?"

Insanely cheap, I told him. Instantly his suspicions were aroused. I said I got the impression that they wanted a quick sale. Again, not entirely truthful; in fact, not truthful at all. I just made that up. I also had concerns about the bafflingly low price, but I was in too deep. That cabinet was going to be mine, come hell or high water.

Dominic wanted to see the actual listing, rather than just the photo I had sent him.

"Why," I snarled, "do you not trust me?"

"Why," he hissed, "are you trying to hide something?"

I flew off the handle, he flew straight after me, and we had a pointless and far-ranging row, encompassing the lid left off the peanut butter, the mix-up over the car's MOT, and some bloke in the restaurant the other night upon whom Dominic's gaze had rested rather too long for my liking.

The next day we made up, as we always did, but the issue lingered, unresolved.

It's not that I thought that he was getting tired of me; I really didn't think that. But, and it sounds ridiculous, but it's true, for almost the first time I was conscious of the age difference. Whereas we had started out as an older, glamorous, successful man and an exciting, slightly dangerous youth, now we were just another bickering old married couple, albeit a May and December match. And he had much more going for him than the odd darling bud; he was a successful man in his own right now, someone courted and consulted, no longer anyone's mentee. And I – well, I was in my prime, still. But maybe not quite the handsome dog of yore. Garlanded with Christmas lights I may have been, but some of the strings had definitely fused.

It's inevitable, I suppose, the slow decline into old age. But I didn't have to rush to meet it. And nor did Dominic. Occasionally these days I had the disagreeable sensation of being managed, or worse, humoured. We'd got into bad habits, of him making decisions and me moaning a bit but basically going along with it, especially after being thrown some kind of sop. Like when I wanted to go to the Amalfi coast, he wanted to go to Florence, and we ended up in a hotel on the Lido with, in my case, mild sunburn, a Bellini hangover and the strong suspicion that Venice had always been his objective. When I stopped and took a long hard look at our lives, I didn't entirely like what I saw.

Hence the cabinet.

He put up a good fight. It wouldn't go with anything. It would stick out like a sore thumb. We'd have to move that sculpture over to make room – and it weighs a ton. Every objection I dismissed or ignored. Finally, Dominic said he had the solution.

An ottoman.

A what?

"It can go at the foot of the bed in the guest room. All the albums can go in there, and there'll still be plenty room to spare. We could use it to store bedding, maybe. Or, I've seen a lovely cashmere throw, that would be nice, in case it turned chilly."

"The guest room."

"I've sourced two that I think would do – a lovely leather one or, if you must indulge this sudden mania for wood, I found a very nice Sheesham design that's Fair Trade. Only two hundred quid."

"I'd still have to kneel on the floor, or bend over to get them out."

"Yes, but –"

"I told you, I want them in the lounge, where I can see them."

"Can't we talk about this?"

"We have talked. We've done nothing but talk. And it's got us nowhere. I've made up my mind. I'm having that cabinet, and it's going in that space."

"Then there's nothing more to be said, is there?"

"No," I said coldly, "there isn't."

I checked the feedback for the seller on the listing site. It was 99% glowing; the single poor review registered was obviously left by a lunatic. I hesitated no longer. I pressed Buy.

Dominic moved into the spare room. I suspect he kicked the storage box as he got into bed. I lay right in the middle of our king-size, luxuriating in the space. But I woke up in the middle of the night feeling suffocated; Mitzi, our cat, was lying on my neck.

"Get off, you stupid animal. Go and annoy your other Dad."

Over breakfast, where both the orange juice and the conversation were strained, I informed Dominic that I had been in contact with the seller and the cabinet would be with us before the weekend. He made no comment. In fact, I had been rather surprised by this myself; I had expected a lengthy negotiation over couriers and handlers and whatnot and was taken aback by the assurances received which were also, I felt, a bit cavalier about the small matter of me being in to receive it. Good job I work from home, I thought grumpily, pushing away the nagging doubts.

That evening Dominic made one last stand; could the cabinet go in the guest room? This was something that had already occurred to me. Looking at the lounge in the pearly late afternoon light and visualising the cabinet in all its barley-twisted glory, I had felt a sudden ripple of unease. It was strong enough to involve taking the tape measure into the spare room and reassuring myself that yes, it would fit in there if we shunted the bed over a bit and moved the small bookcase.

"Certainly not," I said. "It stays in here and so do my records."

Dominic retired early.

"Don't sulk," I said, throwing open the door, "it isn't attractive."

"I'm not sulking," he said, "I'm having an early night."

"It's a quarter to nine," I said.

"So?"

I lingered on the threshold.

"Was there something you wanted?"

"Actually, yes. I want to get the albums out and clean them up, ready for their new home. I anticipate arrival tomorrow. Can you give me a hand?

Between us, we dragged the storage box out from under the bed, with much unnecessary huffing and puffing on his part, and some non-manufactured grunts and wheezes on mine, and then I blew the dust off the top of the container. He sneezed theatrically.

"Anything else?"

"Not that I can think of, offhand."

"I'll bid you good night then."

He shut the door behind me.

I had a glass of twelve-year-old Scotch in one hand and a chamois leather in the other. It should have been blissful, going through the entire collection, re-reading sleeve notes, laughing at obscure messages in the fade-out groove. But actually, I was a bit lonely. Even the damn cat deserted me, heading off, tail held high, in the direction of the spare room. I ended up looking at old YouTube clips of Mott the Hoople. Shutting down the laptop, I noticed some windows had been left open. Dominic had been looking at flats to rent. I didn't sleep too well that night.

He was late home the next evening. I imagine he delayed as much as he possibly could, dreading the awful inevitability and putting it off as long as was humanly possible. He did a double-take as he entered the room, his glance travelling from the wall to me and back to the wall again.

"Why –? Did it not come?"

"Oh yes," I said, "it came. As promised."

"Then what . . . ?"

I handed him the jiffy bag it arrived in. He tipped it up, still mystified and the five-inch, beautifully-crafted piece of doll's house furniture fell out on to his palm.

He stared at it for a good five seconds. Then he started to laugh. Oh, how he laughed. He doubled up with mirth and leant his head on the coffee table. He didn't quite hold his ribs and slap his thighs, he's too cool for that, but he did wipe his streaming eyes. And so did I. I'd already given one short, bitter bark when it was delivered, registered post, but now I gave in and succumbed to the full hilarity.

"How much?" he asked, when he could finally speak.

"I'm not telling you."

"Oh, go on."

So I did, and he doubled up again.

Mitzi took exception to our unseemly display of mirth and wound in between us, rubbing against our sides and batting the empty jiffy bag. Dominic scratched her under her ear, and she started to purr.

"You know," he said, "I could design something. Something that will hold all your vinyl and still look lovely. And also go with everything else in the room."

"But what's the point if you're going to be moving out?"

"I'm not moving anywhere," he said. "I left that stuff out to wind you up."

"Really?"

"Believe me, if I didn't want you to see what I'd been looking at online, you wouldn't ever find it." I recognised the truth of that.

"But," he added, "I do sometimes feel like a lodger."

"After all these years?"

He shrugged. I felt a pinprick of guilt. Hadn't I said, 'After all, it is my flat'? Not *to* him, admittedly, but I had thought it very loudly. To avoid meeting his eye, I announced I was going to make coffee and scuttled off to the kitchen. In the time it took for the percolator to start perking I came to a decision. I arranged the stuff on a tray, along with a plate of biscuits – the good Bahlsen ones that I'd been hiding behind the jar of not-pitted olives, bought in error. He was bent over a sketchpad when I carried it in, ceremoniously.

"Look, I've sketched out an idea. Ooh, nice biscuits. This would be an open shelf for your collection, look; this part would be a storage cupboard, asymmetrical opening, do you see? And these other, smaller shelves could be used to display stuff. Maybe your music books could go there. What do you think?"

I peered at the image. "I think it's lovely. I think you should make it. And I think you should move back into the big bedroom with me." I put my arms around him. "And I think we should put the flat in both our names."

Two months later, I uploaded a photo on to Facebook, captioned 'the new feature'. It attracted many likes and comments about the wonderful, bespoke piece and how good it looked and how it complemented the existing décor. And it really did look good. My albums were arranged there, in all their serried glory; the cupboard hid some useful but unattractive bits and bobs that were good to have on hand but not on show, including my spare reading glasses, Mitzi's worm tablets and a box of man-size tissues for weepie movie nights; one of the shelves held a newly taken photo of Dominic and me in a gorgeous slate frame; another a row of books including my biographies of John Lennon and Lou Reed.

And in the small, central space – the centrepiece, if you like – was displayed a lovingly polished, miniature wooden cabinet – and next to it a tiny gramophone player.

SECOND PRIZE

The Godfather

BY KAREN MCCREEDY

K aren grew up in Staffordshire, and now lives in Bognor Regis after spending twenty years in London.

Her first novel, *Unreachable Skies* was published in 2018 by Mirror World Publishing, and the sequel *Exile* is released in September 2019. Karen is currently working on the third book in this trilogy.

Her first published piece appeared in *Yours* magazine in 1996 and she has since written articles on films and British history for a number of magazines.

Karen's short stories have appeared in various anthologies. Her short story 'Hero' won second prize in *Writers' News* magazine's 'Comeuppance' competition in 2014.

Karen retired in 2018 and when not writing keeps herself busy with many social and volunteering activities. She has even found time to fly in a Spitfire!

Follow Karen on Twitter @McKaren_Writer, or visit her website: www.karenmccreedy.com

The Godfather

BY KAREN MCCREEDY

I've never visited a psychiatrist before – always seen them as expensive props for the wobblier scenery of life – but I've run out of options. There's no-one else I can talk to about this.

You see, I've been … seeing things. Specifically, fairies. I know, I know, it's crazy. That's why I'm here, sitting in a comfy leather arm-chair in the waiting room of London's finest shrink. He must be good, the certificates and photographs are practically double-banked along the walls, and I had to cash in the last of my old company shares to pay his fees, now that I've got no money coming in.

Damn that fairy!

I first saw him about six months ago, though with everything that's happened since then, it seems longer. Back then, I had an office of my own, with a waiting area not unlike this one. I had a beautiful walnut desk, a matching drinks cabinet, a leather swivel-chair with an aroma that broadcast its cost, deep-pile carpet, and the best laptop computer the company's money could buy. I had a beautiful and efficient secretary – the latest in a line of, how shall I put this, obliging models – and my office walls were plastered with photographs: me with councillors and MPs, me with captains of industry, me with the Minister of Trade, me … well, anyway, photos that showed any potential customers that I was a man of influence and importance.

And then that wretched fairy appeared – or, rather, disappeared if you could believe his story – and ruined everything.

I'd spent the morning going over our accounts – the official ones that we showed to the Revenue – and they were pretty gloomy. The recession had hit the electronics industry just as hard as everyone else, and demand for our silicon circuits had fallen dramatically. Cuts would have to be made, and I knew exactly where to start: that troublemaker Morris, with his union's demands for pay rises and flexi-time. He wanted a revolution? Well, I'd give him a helping hand with his march – right out of the door.

But as I called up the staff payroll on my computer screen, I heard a high-pitched, muffled yell.

"Oy!"

It was such a strange, squeaky sort of noise that, at first, I dismissed it as a door in need of oiling. Though that couldn't be, because I always insisted on the highest standards of upkeep in my offices, and a squeaky door within earshot of mine would have meant instant dismissal for the maintenance man. Whoever he was.

So I looked around, decided I'd been hearing things, and went back to studying the list of candidates for redundancy.

"Oy! Jackson! Open your desk drawer!"

I felt my pulse (steady), and my forehead (cool, not clammy), wondering whether this was how nervous breakdowns started. Then, to prove to myself that this was nonsense, I pulled open the top drawer of the desk.

"Aaagh!" I pushed my chair back a good six feet as a tiny grey-bearded man in a green felt hat and a tweed suit climbed out of the drawer and trotted across the desk-top to shake his fist at me. Bizarrely, I found myself hoping that his little black boots would not scratch the veneer, then shook my head at my own foolishness, spun my chair around to face out of the window, and massaged my closed eyes. When I opened them, I took a moment to admire the view over the City, and breathed deep – puzzling over a faint smell of woodsmoke and honey – before turning back to my desk.

"I'm still here." My unwanted visitor gave me a wave. He had perched himself on the edge of my laptop, and the cursor on the screen was moving steadily from left to right, courtesy of his rear end, which was resting on the space bar.

"I'm your fairy godfather," he announced, and got to his feet, leaving several lines of blank space on the screen behind him.

"Or rather – I *was*." He looked cross, and tugged at his jacket in a way that was oddly reminiscent of young Morris readying himself for more unreasonable demands about working conditions.

"I don't understand. What … *who* … ?" And why was I going along with this illusion by talking to it?

The illusion talked back, that was the worst of it. He folded his arms, frowned and repeated, "Your fairy godfather. Yes, yes, I know, most people think we're all supposed to be god*mothers*, but we've got equality laws too, you know." He wagged a finger at me as he went on: "Not that you'd know much about equality laws! I've seen the way you treat the women around here. *And* the way you fiddle your expenses, *and* cheat the tax man, *and* …"

"All right, all right! You've made your point."

"No, I haven't." He pulled a tiny folded paper from his inside jacket pocket and flourished it at me.

"Know what this is? My redundancy notice! After two hundred and forty-three years of loyal service, I'm a cutback! An efficiency saving! Fairy liquidation! And it's *your fault*, Johnny Jackson. All. Your. Fault." He crumpled the paper, threw it on the desk, and kicked it over the 'in' tray onto the carpet.

He sounded like a typical worker, blaming management for his own problems. I decided to play along. Maybe if I acknowledged whatever this delusion was, it would go away.

"Assuming for one moment that I believe in you and your story," I said, sitting back and folding my arms, "How on earth could I be responsible for you losing your job? Before today, I didn't even know you existed."

"That's because you're not *supposed* to know," he said, "I'm breaking the rules being here now, but what the heck? I've got nothing to lose, have I? Not now I'm on the scrapheap." He eyed my laptop for a moment, then climbed onto the keyboard and began to pace from one side to the other. 'lokijuhtgrfedwsqa' appeared on my screen, then he changed direction and typed the same thing again in reverse and capital letters.

"Could you not … ?" I extended my hands in a 'please stop' sort of gesture, and the little monster stopped pacing and started jumping up and down.

"Look, you'll damage the keys – or the software – or something … For heaven's sake, do you know how much that thing cost?"

"What do you care?" he said, though at least he did stop his crazed leaping. "You put it on expenses, didn't you?" He looked quite tearful all of a sudden, and he pulled a tiny hanky from his trouser pocket and blew his nose. "See? That's why they're making me redundant."

"What, because I put my laptop on … ?"

"No, you idiot, because that's the sort of thing you do *all the time*." He sniffed, gave his nose a last wipe, and stuffed the hanky back in his pocket. "We've never had to make cutbacks before, but the King's had a lot of problems just lately, what with the Dwarf Wars, the palace burning down, and that messy divorce from Queen Titania. There just isn't enough Fairy Dust to go round any more, so the King decided that only *deserving* cases of you humans should have a fairy godparent. The rest of us …" He sighed, shoved his hands in his pockets and hung his head. I swear even his hat drooped.

"Pensioned off. Given a dandelion clock and pointed in the direction of the Twirly Club. So …" He raised a hand in a forlorn farewell. "Goodbye, Johnny Jackson. I can't say it's been a pleasure, but at least you kept me in nectar. From here on, you're on your own."

With that, he disappeared. I was looking right at him, and he vanished as though he'd never been, the odour of woodsmoke lingering for a moment before drifting away.

I'd hardly had time to shake my head and remind myself that I'd been imagining him when he popped back again, next to the waste-paper basket. He picked up the scrap of crumpled paper he had kicked onto the carpet, and said: "One last thing – young Morris still has *his* fairy godfather. Just thought you should know."

Then he vanished again, and I thought I'd seen the last of him.

So why am I here now at the psychiatrist's?

Well, I decided that my odd encounter must have been the result of working too hard, so I took a holiday. Ten days in Barbados – all on expenses, naturally, since I took both my laptop *and* my secretary – but when I got back, everything started to go wrong. The Revenue and Customs people turned up unannounced; my secretary said she'd had a better offer and gave in her notice; there was a problem with our suppliers, then difficulties with our customers. The firm was haemorrhaging staff and money. And then …

Then Morris won the EuroMillions. On a rollover. Ninety million and change. Damn the man! Only he didn't hand in his notice and leave, as any decent lottery winner would have done. Oh no. He bought me out and gave *me* notice – and when I went to my drinks cabinet to pour myself something to deaden the blow, guess who was inside, squeaking "Told you so!" He dodged the cut-glass decanter I threw at him, tipped his hat, and disappeared for the last time.

The problem is that ever since then I've been imagining that I can see other people's fairy godparents. There was one in the top pocket of the man who bought my Ferrari; another in the handbag of the woman who bought my riverside apartment. There's one over there now, a tiny female in a pink sweater, perched on the receptionist's shoulder.

So I need to talk, preferably to someone whose job is to listen, nod, and tell me soothingly that I've been working too hard. Just so long as he doesn't trot out any of that clichéd nonsense that I "mustn't feel guilty". After all, why should I? None of this is my fault.

Is it?

THIRD PRIZE

Baby Maker 2065

BY JANE LUPINO

Jane lives in West Sussex with her family and a neurotic labradoodle called Stanley.

Since leaving school, Jane has enjoyed an eclectic career path with jobs involving chemicals, horses, books, more horses, children, learner drivers and bicycles in varying degrees.

After being diagnosed with fibromyalgia, she had to make some major life changes. Writing, always a passion, became a form of therapy.

Her novel, *The Hand of the Dark Mage*, aimed at young adults, and the first of a trilogy, is available on Amazon. Alongside short story writing, she is also working on the next two instalments in her trilogy and a stand-alone novel.

Baby Maker 2065

BY JANE LUPINO

'M.A.C. (Male Android Companion) 2050. The ultimate partner/husband. Designed by ETHANDROID Corporation in 2050.

... In a world now drastically depleted of men, since the Last Great War, the Ethandroid Corporation, headed by multi-millionaire Ethan Stevens, has designed an artificial male companion for the millions of lonely women left behind.

He is everything a woman could want; she can choose his looks, personality, skill sets and work abilities. She can decide whether he will be a successful businessman, a home-loving house-husband or just the ultimate 'Pleasure Package'.

These artificial men are very popular and can be downloaded with different 'Apps' as required.

The only thing missing is the ability to have children which, apart from those lucky enough to have a real human man in their lives, is still only achievable through IVF using sperm from a rapidly depleting stockpile...

... Until now ...'

Harry sat on the long leather sofa and stared down at the magazine in front of him. The publication, *Android Today*, held a cover picture of a young-looking man holding a tiny baby. A young woman stood beside him as they both gazed lovingly at the child. The caption read '*The New Baby-Maker 2065 – A MIRACLE in the Making*'. Harry shook his head and turned again to the page that carried the story. It appeared that this new 'droid was capable of not only carrying live sperm, but they had also created it to reproduce its own supply for future use.

Harry continued to stare in amazement. What would they think of next? He smiled; it was just a good job that his own wife, Kym, wasn't interested in having children.

His smile faded slightly. Maybe she'd changed her mind, though. After all, she had hidden this magazine from him, hadn't she? He would never have known anything about it if he hadn't noticed a corner of it sticking out of her drawer in the bedroom.

He stood up suddenly, tossed the magazine on the coffee table and moved to the huge floor-to-ceiling window that spanned the whole apartment front. That's where she was now, he thought, looking down at the sprawling city below. Somewhere out there on her way home.

* * *

He was still standing there a while later when she came in. He didn't move as he heard the front door close and her footsteps coming along the hall. He remained still as he listened to her take her coat off and throw it over the back of the chair as she often did.

"Hi," she said.

Harry stayed where he stood, silent.

"Honey? What's wrong?" Kym moved in behind him and placed her arm around his waist.

Harry moved then. He turned and walked briskly to the low table that sat between the two long, white, leather couches. Without looking at Kym, he picked up the magazine and thrust it towards her.

Kym hesitated before she took it slowly from his trembling hand.

"Well?" he demanded.

Kym looked up at him, her face sad. "I'm so sorry, Harry. I didn't want you to find out like this ..."

"Oh, really? How did you want me to find out? Were you going to wait until you had him installed before you told me? Is that it?"

"No! Of course not." She paused, dropping the magazine back onto the table. "I wanted to talk to you about this. Explain how I feel about it all ..."

"How *you* feel? What about me? What about how *I* feel?" He stared back out of the window. "I do have an 'Emotion' app, remember?" He felt the ducts behind his eyes begin to fill with fluid. "Kym," he said softly as a tear slid down his cheek. "Are you really just going to trade me in for a younger model?"

* * *

Harry hadn't noticed that it had got dark outside. He had the advantage in that he was fitted with night vision sight as well as normal day vision. He glanced around briefly when she called for 'lights on'. Six lamps immediately lit up various parts of the room, but the main ceiling lights remained off, as programmed.

Harry went to sit on the end of the sofa, away from his wife, not wanting to sit close but not wanting to be too far apart.

Lights were on all over the city, little pinpricks of colour within the pale grey glow that was a constant cover above the tall buildings at night.

A while later, Harry stood up and headed for the kitchen. "You'll be hungry now, I expect,"

"Not particularly," Kym replied.

Harry looked at her. "You must eat. Especially if you intend to go ahead with this and have a baby ..."

Kym sighed loudly and closed her eyes. Harry could see she was hurting, probably more than he was, since his feelings were set on a particular level. He had often wished he could feel as much as humans did, but now, at this moment, he was glad he couldn't.

As he moved around the open plan kitchen, he glanced at Kym from time to time. He knew she was unhappy, but he wasn't going to give in. He was her husband. He wasn't about to lose her to some young whipper-snapper no more than a few months old.

He went back into the lounge and placed a plate of food in front of his wife. She looked at it and turned to face Harry.

"I'm sorry," she said. "I'm really not hungry." She stood up and reached out to touch him but stopped, dropping her hand. "I'm tired. I think I'll just go straight to bed. Goodnight."

Harry nodded but didn't say anything. He watched as Kym walked across the room and disappeared into their bedroom. His super hearing heard her get undressed and into bed. She hadn't asked for lights.

Harry looked at the lamp beside the sofa and after a moment went over and turned it off manually. Then he did the same with the others and went back to stand in front of the window. He gazed out for a few minutes, then, with another advantage over humans, he pressed a tiny switch behind his ear and shut down for the rest of the night.

* * *

The next morning, Harry was sitting at the dining table with the magazine in front of him when Kym emerged from the bedroom.

"Shouldn't you be at work?" she asked. Her voice sounded low and hoarse.

"I called in sick," he replied.

She frowned at him. "How can you be sick? You're a robot."

Harry's face darkened. "I am not a robot. I am an android, and an advanced one at that. I can be whatever I say I am."

Kym stared at him. "Okay."

"I have coffee for you here. Please sit down." Harry motioned to the chair opposite him as he pushed the magazine away. Kym walked over and sat down, taking the cup he offered. She took a mouthful of the bitter-sweet liquid.

"It's cold!"

"Oh, sorry." Harry took the mug and held it tight between his hands. After a few seconds, steam began to rise from the cup and he handed it back.

"Thank you," said Kym.

She drank in silence for a moment, Harry watching her.

"We should talk," he said, still gazing unblinkingly at his wife.

Kym just nodded, staring into her coffee cup.

"When did you decide you wanted a baby?" asked Harry.

Kym looked up. Her face was pale, and there was uncertainty deep in her eyes. "I-I'm not sure," she said. "I'm not even sure I do."

Harry stayed silent, waiting for her to continue.

"I was with some friends one day, and we saw a woman with a baby. They're so rare we all fussed over it a little, and I just mentioned that it might be quite nice to have a child."

Harry still said nothing.

Kym carried on. "Well, the other day, Jem gave me the magazine. She said that I should take a look at it, so I did."

Harry looked thoughtful for a moment. "And now how do you feel about it?"

Kym bit her lip. Her eyes shone with tears in the harsh morning light coming in through the big windows. "I never wanted IVF, you know that. In fact, I'm dead against it; you hear so many stories about things going wrong. And then there was that scare when everyone thought they were using human women to have animal babies or whatever... Well, I don't want to get involved." She paused and looked up at Harry. "Besides, I wasn't ready for a baby then. But now ..."

"Now?"

Kym blinked back the tears. "Now, I think I'd like to have one," she whispered.

Harry stared at his hands. He nodded his head and took a deep breath. "I see. So, it's out with the old and in with the new then ..."

"No! No, Harry, of course not." She reached out for his hand. His sensors felt the warmth of her skin, and he turned his palm up against hers.

"Harry," she continued. "We've been together for fifteen years. We had a wedding ceremony. You don't just forget that and start again."

"So, what do we do then?" His eyes were clear, cold.

He'd turned down his emotion app quite low.

Kym shook her head slowly and squeezed his hand. "I don't know. I just don't know."

"If you trade me in, they'll wipe my memory and clear all my downloads. I'll be a blank shell again until someone else takes me." He paused. "I will forget everything, forget you, us. Everything. It'll be like we never were."

Tears flowed down Kym's face. "I could never do that. I couldn't bear it!"

Harry got up and went to his favourite spot in front of the window. Kym stayed seated, her hands folded and her head low. Harry looked over his shoulder at her. She seemed so small sitting there, so frail. If he had had a heart, it would've broken at the sight of her.

He went over and knelt beside her. "I love you, Kym. And I want to make you happy. I can change. I'll do anything for you. Just please, please don't exchange me." He stood up and glanced at the magazine.

He turned and strode across the room and out into the hallway. Without a word he opened the front door and headed for the lift.

*　*　*

He had managed to get an appointment at eleven-thirty that morning. He sat now in a large reception room. Several comfortable chairs lined the peach-coloured walls, and low, square tables were dotted around, each with papers and magazines spread out on them. A tall water cooler stood in one corner. A receptionist sat at a low desk beside the entrance to a long corridor. She was probably human since there were very few female androids about, but this was the Ethandroid Corporation after all, so anything was possible.

She seemed totally engrossed in her work and had hardly even acknowledged Harry's presence, but now she suddenly looked up and smiled at him.

"Mr Stevens will see you now, sir. Just down the hall, last door on the left," she said, pointing down the corridor.

Harry stood up and went along the hallway. He reached the door and knocked twice (he had the latest 'Manners' app after all) and went in.

Mr Stevens was a tall, thin man. He stood on the other side of a huge wooden desk that filled half of the office. Tall bookcases lined one wall and the books on them looked real, a rarity in these days. Two high-backed chairs were on Harry's side of the desk, and he moved towards one, holding his hand out to shake with Mr Stevens'.

Stevens ignored the hand as he came around the desk staring intently at Harry. "My God!" he whispered. "You're an early edition 'MAC'. I can tell by the skin texture, but you look … amazing!" He circled around behind Harry, still scrutinising him.

Harry frowned and tried to shuffle around following Stevens. The man's face was so close to Harry that he almost brushed noses with him.

Stevens stood back a fraction, still staring. "Well, well. I thought all the first editions were gone now, but obviously not. What are you, ten, twelve years old?"

Harry raised his eyebrows. "I'm an original 2050, sir. Fifteen years old, one lady owner."

Mr Stevens went back behind his desk, nodding his head. "Yes. Well, she's certainly taken very good care of you." He sat down and gestured for Harry to do the same.

Stevens leaned forward. He shook his head, still smiling. "Well then, what is it I can do for you?"

Harry cleared his throat. He didn't need to, but he'd seen humans do it before saying something important, so he did it too. "It's about the Baby-Maker 2065s."

"Ah, yes, 'F.R.EDs'. Aren't they something? Now any woman who wants a baby can have one the natural way. No more of this IVF stuff, just plain old-fashioned ... reproduction!"

"Sorry, who's 'Fred'?"

"F.R.ED, that's what we call them: Fertile Reproductive EDition. Good eh?"

"Oh, um. Yes. Very good." Harry paused, frowning slightly. "Well, what I want to know is ..." He paused. He wasn't quite sure how to put it. "Well, does a woman have to have a 'Fred'? I mean, if she still wants a baby."

"As I said, there's the IVF programme, if she qualifies, of course."

"Qualifies?"

"Well, yes. She'd have to be within the age limits and be healthy and fit. Preferably intelligent too. After all, if we're going to breed human males, we want them to be strong *and* clever."

"Do these limits apply to the baby ... I mean 'Fred' too?"

"Well, obviously the younger, healthier women will be the first choice; we can't take too many chances. After all, these machines are very expensive and ..."

"So not every woman who wants one will get one?"

"Not straight away, no. Not until we can produce enough to go around, and I can't see that being for a few more years yet."

"I see. Well, my wife, Kym, she's healthy and very intelligent ..." He stared at the top of the desk for a moment. "You see, she wants a baby and I'm afraid she's going to trade me in for a ... a ... well, a 'Fred'. But the thing is I don't want to be traded in. Or stripped down ready to go on to another owner ..."

"Oh, I don't think you'd go to someone else," interrupted Mr Randall.

Harry brightened a little. "No?"

"No. You're far too old for that. I'm afraid you'd be looking at the scrapheap, my friend. Sorry."

"What? No!" Harry was horrified.

Mr Stevens leaned forward again, his eyes narrowing. "Wait a minute. Are you telling me you *care* about what happens to you?"

"Yes."

"You're actually *worried* about your future?"

"Yes!"

Stevens leaned back, tapping his fingers on the desktop, still staring at Harry. "But you're an android. You're not built to worry about things like that."

Harry thought about that for a moment. "Well, *I* am."

"How?"

"I ... I have a 'Care' app. Kym bought it for me years ago."

"'Care' apps are to make you care about other beings ..."

"I do ... but I care about myself as well."

Stevens was thoughtful for a while. He stood up suddenly. "Come with me," he said.

Harry followed him out of the office and back down the long hallway. As they reached the second door from Reception, Stevens opened a door and started to descend a flight of stairs. They continued down for several floors until Stevens led Harry through another door and into a large spacious room filled with strange machines. They walked past several units where people were working and finally stopped beside a large machine, which blinked with a vast array of lights.

A small plump man was working there, and he stopped when Stevens and Harry appeared.

"Wait here." Stevens told Harry as he pulled the plump man aside.

A few moments later, the men turned back to Harry. "Dr Feltz here is going to see what's going on in your processor."

"What?" Harry took a step back.

"Don't worry, it won't hurt. It's just a scan to see how you're operating," explained the doctor.

Harry looked from him to Stevens and back. Dr Feltz beckoned Harry over to a low glass-topped table.

Harry went over and sat in a chair beside the table. Feltz reached over and placed a small unit against a spot behind Harry's ear.

After a few moments, images appeared in the space above the table. Feltz studied the images for a moment then turned to Stevens and Harry.

"Well," he said. "It seems our friend here is rather unique."

Harry frowned at Mr Randall.

Feltz went on. "Your 'Care' app seems to have fused into your main computer and is now an integral part of your make-up. It's become part of you." He paused. "And it's growing."

"What?" Stevens exclaimed. "How?"

Feltz smiled at Harry, who by now was as confused as ever. "Your capacity for learning has expanded beyond all our built-in parameters. All apps downloaded have become integral, a part of you, just like ..."

"A human ..." said Stevens, stunned.

* * *

Later that night, Harry entered the apartment and found Kym lying on the sofa asleep. As he went to her, she awoke.

"Oh, Harry, where have you been?"

Harry smiled at her. He held out a piece of paper to her.

"What is it?" Kym asked, looking puzzled.

"I told you I could change," Harry replied.

Kym opened the paper and read it.

> **"This certificate is proof of upgrade from M.A.C 2050;**
> **serial no. 2741963/B7zd to F.R.ED, 2065(BABY-MAKER)**
> **serial no. 000001/A0. The first and only of his kind."**

Kym looked up at Harry. "Oh, Harry ..."

"I thought you could call me Fred now," he said and kissed his wife.

HIGHLY COMMENDED

Michel's Smile

BY JOHN MARSTON

Whilst having been involved in the creative arts for most of his life – organising an annual arts festival in the West Country, teaching English, and running a theatre department at Queen's College, Taunton – John has only focused more fully on his own creative writing in the last year or so. He is interested in how the pressure for social conformity affects the individual, and the effect of technology on modern life.

Michel's Smile

BY JOHN MARSTON

I've become good at smiling or at least appearing to smile, and I can laugh too if I work the facial muscles the right way. Some people don't smile back.

I'm on a bus outside the city, and we're heading to the destination. It's a forty-mile trip from here. Anyone watching this little group, tightly packed into the bus, would simply see an elderly man, accompanied by his daughter and granddaughter. I'm smiling at my granddaughter. My daughter had insisted that I accompany her. I'm reassuring my granddaughter that she has nothing to fear. That's why I'm doing the smiling bit. I'm alright, really I am, my smile says, and you are too. I think I mentioned the bus was crowded.

So as I said we're on the bus leaving the city; it is starting to snow. It always seemed to be snowing here. People are saying it's warm on the bus, but as I look around at our fellow travellers, I feel cold.

There are a few family groups on the bus, most of them looking serious. Quite a few don't have seats. There is one other family group that I particularly notice. It consists of a boy, about twelve years old, roughly the same age as my granddaughter, and what I take to be his grandparents. The boy is clearly well brought up. You can always tell. He looks quite old-fashioned and earnest as well, what with his neat black hair and the top button of his shirt done up. It is, as I mentioned, crowded. There is no doubt that he respects his elders and I am surprised he is sitting while his grandfather stands next to them. I try out my smile on the grandmother, and she smiles back. Our smiles say, "We're proud of our grandchildren. They are here because of us." The grandfather looks at me but doesn't join in the smiling.

After about twenty minutes or so into the trip, the boy begins to get restless. The grandmother smiles indulgently and kisses the top of his head, and then puts her arm protectively around him to make him more comfortable. Love is important for people. He leans his head against his grandmother and is soon asleep. The grandfather regards me, then looks down intently at his family; he is still not smiling.

Anyway, after forty minutes, we arrive at Lajkonik, which is only a few miles from Oswiecem. We are told, ordered really, that we needed to be back on the bus, at the same spot in two hours or we might not make it back. Two hours would give us plenty of time for the tour. I've always been fearful about getting instructions wrong, probably because I like to follow the rules.

It's snowing harder now, but we do the tour. You may have done it yourself, or you may know people who have. I wouldn't have gone, but as I said earlier, I am there for my daughter and granddaughter. Halfway around, the need to leave becomes overwhelming. I knew it would, but word has by then spread of my presence, and I become, for a while, the focus of interest. I speak to a group of tearfully attentive Norwegians. I talk to them about some of the facts but nothing else. I don't cry. I haven't since the day I first left this place. I know it would have helped my daughter if I did; she and her generation are great believers in something they call 'closure'. I've been crying in my heart for seventy years of course, and will until I die. My granddaughter is tearful too, and I do my best to comfort her with my smile. I persuade her and my daughter, as I am tiring, to meet me outside the main entrance when they have finished. We've come a long way, I tell them, and it's important that they take their time. Not me though. I need to be outside in the cold.

So here I am, waiting outside the red brick walls, and I can see the railway line, and thankfully I'm alone. Alone with the snow. I look back, and I can see that my footprints are being filled in. Soon my tracks will be gone. I am so very tired, and I feel the need to sit down. I find a bench. It's a relief to sit.

The railway lines are very close to where I'm sitting, and further down the line I can make out a truck. I remember having my wish granted.

Seventy years ago, on a truck like that, I wasn't able to sit down, not at first anyway. We couldn't because there were no seats, just two buckets in each of the train's cattle trucks. More humans could be packed in without seats. As the train had made its way to Krakow people died on the way, but you know that. There had been no water or food on the journey, but you probably also know that and that the elderly perished first. The dead were carted off at the stops. That you might or might not have known. On the last leg from Krakow to Oswiecem, I'd had my wish granted. I had been able to sit.

Truth is more important than tears. So listen to the truth and forgive me. I had to sit down to survive that journey. If I was to stand any longer, I knew I would die.

You hear me, but still, you don't understand. How can you? Listen. It had been my wish that others should die so that I could sit down. I was a boy then of about twelve years old and had been widely thought to have been well brought up, but this boy I talk of was fervently praying that people might die, so he could sit. God grants some wishes and denies others. This one he granted. One elderly man on the train had been close to death, and it was I who killed him. He'd only been able to remain standing because he was so tightly pressed up against us, supported by us. I was pushed face to face with him. As our skeletons dug into each other, we were forced into an embrace, and as we embraced, I prayed for his death. I prayed and prayed.

God heard my prayers. His breath was on my cheek for hours, irregular and faint, and we swayed together in our dance until his breath stopped. He died standing up, pushed tightly against me. We remained in this clinch for the rest of the journey. I don't remember his smell and I don't remember his sounds but I do remember regretting that he'd only briefly been warm in death. By the time we'd reached Krakow, he had turned stiffly cold. It was difficult to become unentangled; we'd become fused. Of course, we still are. I could easily have been taken away with him, and would have been, if we hadn't been ordered to separate the dead from the living ourselves. On the way to Oswiecem, which I've already told you is only forty minutes from Krakow, I was finally able to sit on the carriage floor.

So here I am outside the red brick walls, close to the railway line, waiting. My family find me sitting on the bench, and I can see that they have been crying. Behind them are the rest of the group. We drift back to the bus together with my granddaughter leaning into my arm. Not much, if anything, is said as we get back on the bus for the journey back to Krakow. I'll be at my hotel in an hour. If I'm alone there, I might get warm.

We all sit in the same seats because we've left belongings on the bus, umbrellas and so forth. We were told to leave our things there. We were told that they would be there when we got back on the bus. The bus fills up silently as people are checked off and we prepare for the journey back to Krakow. Opposite me, I see the boy again. I'm pleased to see him. He's leaning his head against his grandmother's shoulder, and I can see he's been crying even though his eyes are shut, but he's safe, and he's on the bus heading away from here. It's good they both have seats. Everyone has one now, and no one is left standing. It's not crowded on the way back as it was on the way here. I look further down the aisle in search of the old man. As I thought, he's not on the bus. No-one apart from me notices this, neither the grandmother nor the boy, nor anyone else. I don't need to tell anyone. How could they possibly understand? I know that I'll see him, the old man that is, at some point in any day, stiffly standing and unsmilingly looking at me. Sometimes I feel his breath on me. I always sense his coming when the cold takes hold of me and wraps its blanket around me in a shroud. He could appear anywhere, but now on this return trip to Krakow, there is no sign of him, and I find myself wanting – needing – to see him. If he appears, I'll try my smile on him, but I know he won't smile back. I'll keep working on my smile until he does. I see him every day: on the streets, in cafes, even in my own house, and of course on the trains.

HIGHLY COMMENDED

Forward Planning

BY DAVID WARWICK

David comes originally from the Meon Valley, Hampshire, but now lives in Chichester, and has written all his life, both for the press and radio. As a university lecturer in this country, and as a professor in Russia, he was the author of some forty non-fiction books and for many years was indexer of *Whitaker's Almanack*. His first novel, *Chorus Endings*, was recently published by Matador and he is now working on a second.

Forward Planning

BY DAVID WARWICK

"So, no matter what business we're in, strategic thinking is vital." As the interpreter cut in on cue Mike added a final arrow – crimson and purposeful – to the diagram he'd constructed and readied himself for the punchline.

Gathering up his notes he made as if to leave, but then – almost as an afterthought – leant across the lectern, casually polishing his glasses. "There are only three things you need to remember about running a successful company – forward planning, forward planning, forward planning!" The translation was followed by a moment's silence; then an excited babble, some puzzled laughter and a paroxysm of frenzied scribbling, during which Mike made his escape. Muffling himself up against the bitter chill and trudging out over the gangplank, he wondered: were the lectures as effective here as they had been elsewhere? Certainly they had sounded terrific in Russian and no one could accuse him of insincerity. This current itinerary, for instance: a businessman's cruise sandwiched neatly between consultancies in Kansas and Toronto, enabling him to complete his manuscript before summer schools in Lisbon and Helsinki – all had been most carefully thought through. So, too, was the way he had restricted his drinking and followed doctor's orders regarding the headaches and bad dreams. It was all down to forward planning.

A sudden flurry of snow brought Mike to a halt. It was difficult to estimate how far he'd walked but now the indistinct shape of a large building loomed up ahead. Between whirling flakes he made out a cupola, onion-shaped and luminous in the half-light, minarets tapering into the larger darkness; closer to hand, angular tombstones, the outline of skeletal metal crosses. His flashlight, playing on the nearest of these, caught a shallow inscription and, above it, the customary portrait, stained and faded with age. It was that of a young woman; one who seemed strangely familiar to him. She must have been aged nineteen or twenty. Laughing eyes; lips parted in a shy smile; high, almost oriental cheekbones; black hair tumbling onto delicate shoulders; the beginnings of a blush caught on camera. How well he knew her, and yet …

"Mikhail!" A whisper amid the rustling of the leaves. Mike spun round, but there was no one there.

Again the voice – soft as snow, sharp as ice – "At last you have come, Mikhail."

"Is that you, Tamara?"

A peal of light, seductive laughter, again behind him – or was it inside his head?

"The waiting has been long, Mikhail, but our loving is forever. Wait for me at Suzdal." One last word, this time from a great distance, "Sudba!" and her voice was lost in the sighing of the wind.

Alone again, Mike turned his attention to the inscription. Scraping away ice and frozen lichen, he traced its faded outline in the corroded metal. One word only was decipherable: *Tamara*. Just how had he known her name?

For what seemed like an eternity he stood transfixed, then laughed out loud. Alone among the tombstones, in a blizzard, late at night, thousands of miles from home, yet deep down inside – and for the first time in years – he felt neither loneliness nor fear.

* * *

"To summarise, then: structure, perspective, proportion. These are the key elements of any endeavour, whether it's running a company, building a church or organising your life." Mike brought the Yaroslavl slide clearly into focus and, to a ripple of applause, subsided into his chair. "An excellent analogy," the interpreter assured him later over a drink, "a fortuitous one, too. As I told them, tomorrow we can verify your words, in the Cathedral of the Nativity at Suzdal. So, here's to coincidence." He raised his glass. "Or perhaps *sudba* would be more appropriate?" he added. "Now, how do you say that in English? Yes, of course, it's *Kismet* or *Fate*!"

* * *

The Cathedral – triple-storied, domed and cruciform – amply justified his metaphor, but Mike hardly noticed this. She was with him almost continually now: individual features only vaguely remembered, but the sound of her voice, the ripple of her laughter clear in his mind whilst, beyond the threshold of consciousness – timeless and elusive – stirred memories of quite a different kind. Bounding up the six shallow steps, Mike took his place impatiently alongside other tourists entering the great Western Gate. Inside: shuffling feet, priestly intonations, murmured responses; the rise and fall of voices in disembodied chant. A thousand or more guttering candles brought icons, dark and brooding, flickering to life. Overpowered by the scent of musk, leather, old parchment, Mike staggered backward and, as he did so, felt a hand, cool and gentle, placed in his. He turned. Tamara's face was a few inches away, her body close to his. Mike bent towards her, but she placed her fingers against his lips.

"Not yet, Mikhail," she breathed. Then, with a smile, "Christmas, my love, I will be with you then. For always. I promise."

Tamara detached herself from his embrace and backed slowly away. Briefly she paused before the gold-encrusted altar, smiled, blew him a kiss and was lost amid swirling clouds of incense.

*   *   *

On his return Mike threw himself into his work with renewed vigour. Writing, lecturing, consultancy, workshops, anything to keep Tamara from his mind; anything to bring Christmas that much closer.

He booked a small Cornish cottage, miles off the beaten track, having neither phone nor e-mail, and locked his laptop in the office cupboard. Then, with a fridge full of Christmas dinners, a crateful of whisky, setting up the tree and turning on the fairy-lights, he at last gave himself over to waiting for the girl in the photograph.

But she did not come. Neither that night nor on Christmas Day. Still Mike did not give up hope. Tamara had promised and, deep in his heart, he just knew she would be there.

As the New Year approached he became increasingly desperate. Huddled continually before the television, unshaven and haggard, his only exercise became visits to the slowly emptying crate and more frequent journeys to a dustbin now overflowing with bottles.

New Year's Day and the subsequent week passed in this fashion when Mike became dimly aware that Twelfth Night – Christmas' grand finale

– was upon him. Give her till then, he thought, still convinced that she would not break her promise.

But midnight found him slouched besides the smartly decorated tree, lonely and demoralised, whilst – oblivious to his misery – the television played on. Concentrating for one last time on the girl he loved to distraction, Mike took a final gulp from the bottle, placed the gun in his mouth and pulled the trigger.

"Now," intoned the television anchor-man as the fairy lights continued to flash, "we say 'Good-bye London,' and 'Hello Moscow', where the choir of St Basil's are on hand to welcome in this first day of the Russian Christmas."

Her laughter fills the room. "Mikhail, I am here," she calls, "just as I promised," and, as Mike rises to his feet, an excited Tamara quite literally melts into his arms. Hours, days, years, or is it centuries, pass before, momentarily, he withdraws from her embrace.

"Sudba," he whispers.

"Forward planning," sighs a very contented Tamara.

CAROLINE TRAVIS

Caroline has two stories in this anthology. Current members of the Bognor Regis Write Club were allowed to enter up to three stories. Our members did not get a free pass – all stories were judged anonymously, and still had to make it into the judges' top five to make it into the book.

So, let me introduce you to the first of our members. She was also a judge but, needless to say, did not judge her own work.

When Caroline is not writing quirky, sharply observed domestic fiction, she is enjoying life by the seaside and renovating her current home. She works closely with Julia Macfarlane on projects such as this short story competition, where she was fellow judge and co-editor. She has had stories published in *A Blast On The Waverley's Whistle*; *The View From Here*; and *Chichester Ghost Tour*.

Not Today

BY CAROLINE TRAVIS

THURSDAY EVENING:

Stanley picked up his phone and studied the keys like they held the meaning of life. He gently pressed the contacts button; only one name appeared. His unsteady hand touched the name and Kate's image smiled at him. The green handset icon beckoned and Stanley's finger obeyed. He counted the rings.

"Hi, Pops."

"Kate, love. I'm sorry to bother you." His voice trembled slightly.

"Are you okay? What's up?"

"I – I've had a bit of a fall."

"I'll be straight round. Are you hurt?"

"I don't think so, love. I'm just a bit shaken up."

Kate was already looking for her car keys as she disconnected the call. "Ella?" She shouted up the stairs. "Ella!"

"Ella's at Helen's," Nick called from the kitchen. "Why?"

"Oh, yes. Of course she is. Look, Stan's had a fall."

"What? No, not now." Nick's eyes moved skyways as he held onto the words he wanted to say. "I'll come with you."

When Stanley saw Kate's car pull into the close he made his way, as quickly and carefully as he could, to the living room where he gently lowered himself down onto the floor, and as he heard the front door key slide into the lock, he replaced the little smile with a small frown.

"Pops?" cried Kate, as she pushed the front door open.

"In here." He swallowed. "In here," he repeated, more feebly.

Kate hurried down the hallway, across the lounge, and knelt next to the prone figure. "What you doing down here then, Pops?"

"You'll be tickling his belly next," mocked Nick from the doorway.

"Who's that?" Stanley barked.

Kate flinched. "It's Nick, Pops. You know Nick." A puzzled frown crossed her brow.

"Where's Ella?" he demanded, petulantly.

"Your granddaughter is – busy. Nick thought I might need a hand to get you up. So ..."

Stanley pushed his elbow back onto the sofa and started to raise himself up.

Kate smiled. "Whoa. Steady on, tiger." She placed her feet in front of his, fixed her hands to his elbows, and using her own body weight, she slowly levered him to his feet.

He took a step back and sat down. "You'll stay for a cup of tea, won't you?"

"How come," Nick's slow words drew the attention of the other two. "You're on the floor over there, and your phone," he paused, "is on the kitchen worktop?" He reached through the door and picked up the offending article.

"I – I –" Stanley put his head in his hands and rubbed his eyeballs. He raised his head to his accuser. "I tripped in the kitchen." He turned back to Kate, nodding slightly. "Crawled in here to see if I could use the sofa to help me up."

"Do you hurt anywhere?" She looked him over. "Perhaps you should come home with ..."

"Or perhaps we should start looking for a nursing home," Nick stonewalled.

"No, no. Really. I'm fine now." He shuffled forward. "Nice strong cup of tea should do it."

"I'll put the kettle on," smiled Nick, leaving the door ajar as he went.

Stanley looked at the slightly open kitchen door and frowned. "I'm really not sure about that one, love. Our Kevin, he *will* come back – soon as he comes to his senses?"

Kate smiled indulgently. "Nick's a good man, Pops, and he loves Ella to bits. *Our* Kevin, as you put it, chose a different path a while ago now and I'm pretty sure he's not going to be crawling back in our direction any time soon. He doesn't even send his daughter birthday cards. In fact ..."

"Tea up," sang Nick as he waltzed back into the room, mug in hand.

"You not having one then?"

"Apparently not." Kate was as surprised as her ex-father-in-law.

Nick placed the cup beside the old man and looked at his watch like a commando synchronising his piece. "We have to be somewhere at eight. It's twenty to now, so if you're alright ..."

"Oh yes," Kate's hand touched her forehead at the forgotten memory. "The rehearsal."

"What?"

"Nick's sister, Helen, is getting married on Saturday. The church rehearsal is tonight." She looked at the clock on the mantel and turned to Nick. "Do you think she'll mind if ..."

"You *promised* her." Nick turned the screw a little more.

"Look, Pops. I really have to go – if you're sure you're alright."

Stanley's complexion had greyed a little and he started to rub the small of his back. "I – I'll be fine. You get along, love. No point wasting your time on an old codger like me."

"I'll pop in tomorrow," Kate murmured guiltily. "Make sure you're okay." She stood up and bent to kiss the old man on the forehead. "Don't get up, we'll see ourselves out and I'll see you tomorrow."

Stanley watched as Nick placed his hand in the small of Kate's back, guiding her away. Neither saw Stanley stand up as nimbly as a fifty-year-old. He made his way to the window and, as he watched the car pulling out of the drive, he murmured; "Don't you go catching any flying bouquets, young lady."

"You know he's playing you, don't you?"

Kate kept her eyes on the road. "He's just lonely and he's been really good to Ella and me since ..."

"But that's the third time in a fortnight. Last week," his left hand seized his right forefinger for emphasis, "it was his toilet cistern. Ella said you couldn't find anything wrong with it."

"To be fair, I told him how to fix it when he called."

"Last weekend," Nick continued, imprisoning another digit. "He couldn't get any hot water, and you found he'd managed to switch off the power to the boiler."

"That was an accident – when he was cleaning."

"What? Like the accident he had this evening." Nick's hands flew apart as his shoulders hunched.

"He's in his eighties, Nick."

"And he has a son."

"He doesn't talk to Kevin since …" Again, Kate couldn't bring herself to finish the sentence.

"… Since Kevin ran off with his boyfriend," Nick tried to keep his tone prosaic.

Kate winced, indicated left and pulled into the church car park, her troubled frown melting into a warm and sunny smile as Nick's three-year-old daughter, Kylie, ran towards the car.

SATURDAY MORNING:

Stanley was standing at his kitchen window, studying the overhanging branches of next-door's fir tree, as he had every morning for the last week, and felt the bile rise. The new incumbents next door had pruned their side of the tree last Saturday, but because Stanley had been out at the time, they hadn't bothered to trim any of the rampaging mass heading in his direction.

"We couldn't reach them," David had whined, "and you weren't answering the door."

"Of course I wasn't answering the flaming door – I was OUT." And now, the numbskull was gallivanting abroad, sunning himself on some foreign beach. Well, enough was enough.

Stanley selected his loppers and pruning saw from the shed. First, he clipped back anything he could reach from the ground which, he thought, 'was of damned little use'. He tried extending the loppers to their full length, but he just couldn't get enough muscle behind the handles to cut anything.

He backed away, still looking at the tree, trying to judge if he might find a purchase for the ladder, and bumped into the old, teak garden table. He looked from one to the other a couple of times.

"Hmm." he murmured as he placed a plastic chair on the top.

"Maybe." He turned his back to the table, lifted his backside onto the slatted, wooden top and swung his legs. It seemed stable enough. He manoeuvred himself, using the chair for support, into standing, but before he had quite steadied himself the chair slipped, and one of the legs skated into the gap between the wooden slats, leaving it fixed at a forty-five-degree angle.

"You cretinous imbecile," he admonished from his elevated position. "Witless idea," he continued as he climbed down. Shaken, he took himself inside for a strong cup of coffee and a smoke.

As Stanley lit his roll-up, Kate and Nick were leaving the eager bridesmaids at Helen's. Kate gave Ella a hug and fiddled with a strand of stray hair. "You're going to need a bit more hairspray, and keep an eye on Kylie, she seems a bit fretful."

"Go home, and get ready, Mum. I'm fine, and she's fine."

Kate kissed her daughter on the forehead. "See you in church, then."

"Just go, Mum."

Nick laughed as he watched Ella push her mum out of the door.

As Nick and Kate arrived back at Kate's to ready themselves for Helen's big day, Stanley cussed and cursed in his battle to release his ladder from its supporting pegs.

"I'll do it for you next weekend, Stan," Stanley mimicked the neighbour.

"Just have a little patience, old man," he lampooned as he struggled down the garden.

"I'll give him old man." Stanley settled his ladder and got on with the job in hand. Each bit he cut, he aimed, like a five-year-old with a paper plane, into David's perfect garden.

Stanley was just beginning to enjoy his task as Kate put the finishing touches to her own hair and Nick was still singing in the shower when Kate's phone rang.

"Ella? What's up?"

"Mum, it's Kylie. She's ruined her hair and won't let the hairdresser anywhere near her. Apparently, only Auntie Kate can do it. Helen's well stressed."

"Man!" Katie sighed loudly.

"Can you hear her?" Kylie was nearing hysteria in the background.

"Okay. I'm getting in the car now," Kate said, as she hung up and hurriedly loaded a small bag with her make-up, accessories and hair-dressing essentials.

While Kate quickly explained the situation to Nick, Stanley looked at his progress and gave a satisfied grunt. He'd cleared all the branches to his left and as far to the right as he could reach until he went a little too far and his body felt a slight movement in the ladder. He snapped back to the upright and held it tight until his heart rate returned to normal and he'd thought about his next move. He could go down and move the ladder, or, he could go up and climb on top.

He pulled himself up another couple of rungs and grabbed hold of an up-standing fir tuft. He gave it a substantial tug. Still clinging to the tree, he pulled himself up one more step, found a branch for his right foot and pulled himself up onto the crown. As his left foot pushed off, the ladder went crashing to the ground.

Stanley clung to the foliage until his heart stopped palpitating, and slowly manoeuvred himself into an upright sitting position. His eyes swept the gardens, but he could see no movement.

"Hello!" he shouted through cupped hands in one direction.

He turned his head in the opposite direction.

"Hello?" He waited for another moment. "Can anyone hear me?"

He looked for a way of climbing down but swiftly recognised that plan's futility.

"For pity's sake," he grumbled and pulled out his mobile phone.

As Stanley was counting the rings, Nick was buttoning his shirt in front of Kate's full-length mirror.

"Help! I need somebody." Nick stopped and listened.

"Help! Not just anybody." Nick started walking to the landing.

"Help! You know I need someone. He-e-elp!"

Nick lent over the bannister.

"Hello?" he called into the beat of silence.

As the sequence began again, Nick's face creased into a grin at the memory of changing the old man's ringtone on Kate's mobile. By the time it had ended, he'd reached the disremembered phone, his smile had slithered into a scowl; and with just a splinter of guilt, he slid the device under a magazine.

"Oh, no, you don't, Stan, not today."

JULIA MACFARLANE

Julia s a founder of Aldwick Publishing and Bognor Regis Write Club. Her own short stories explore business life, personal lives and impossible situations with dark wit and well-drawn characters. She also produces anthologies of stories and poems with fellow Sussex writers, and has compiled the popular Chichester Ghost Tour, for which private tours can be booked via bognorwriters@gmail.com.

All her books can be found on Amazon and in local book shops. They include:

A Blast On The Waverley's Whistle (Bognor Write Club anthology 2016)
The View From Here (Bognor Write Club Anthology 2017)
Chichester Ghost Tour
News of Leon & Other Tales (Collection of her own short stories)

Apart from creating the book in your hands, she is currently co-editing *A Feast of Christmas Stories* to be published in October 2019 with fellow writers from CHINDI, the network of Independent Authors.

Find out more at her website: www.macfarlanejuliawriter.com.

The Hour Glass

BY JULIA MACFARLANE

Margot Trent is dying.

Here, in this quiet side-room, on the first floor of the hospice, on the outskirts of her home town, Margot's last few hours are counting down. The only sounds are her long, slow breaths, not quite a struggle but with a rasp each time, suggesting effort. One of her hands twitches convulsively, plucking at the white hospital sheet, and her eyes stare out towards the sunlit windowsill and its contents.

Lisa, a woman past middle-age herself, holds the other hand lightly in hers as she sits next to the bed, keeping vigil over her dying mother.

The door opens and Glynis, the end-of-life nurse (a ghastly job title that Lisa had had no idea existed until Glynis had introduced herself yesterday), pops her head around. Glynis of the soft brown hair, softly wrinkled face and soft-soled shoes, says in her soft, sing-song voice:

"Hello, there, Mrs Trent. And Lisa, are you still here? Now, have you been home for a shower and a rest since I saw you yesterday? Because you must look after yourself as well, you know."

Lisa gives a short shake of her head. "Once my brother's here, I'll take a break." Glynis raises a gentle eyebrow and Lisa adds, "I promise."

"Now, Mrs Trent, or do you think your mum would prefer Margot?" Glynis pronounces Margot more like 'maggot" and Lisa winces.

"It's pronounced 'Margoh'." Lisa has a rush of memory: schoolfriends' shuffling feet in their tiny kitchen – 'Mrs Trent, Mrs Trent, could we have a glass of water, please?' And Mum saying: 'Please, call me Margot, Mrs Trent sounds like an old woman! And we can do better than water, can't we, Lisa?' There was always a welcome

58

in the Trent family home. And now here Margot is, very much an old woman … "My mum would much prefer you call her Margot."

"I am sorry, Margot. Silly me, and it's such a lovely name. Just like all these knickknacks Lisa has brought from home for you."

Family photos in ornate frames, a paperweight where silver bubbles hang eternally suspended in a purple sea, a few china dogs and cats, jostle for place amongst a tissue box, disposable glove packets, sponges for moistening dry lips – and dominating the windowsill between two vases of fresh flowers:

"Now that has to be the biggest egg-timer I have ever seen! Is it for boiling an ostrich egg?"

Lisa laughs, and Glynis encourages her with a little nod and a gesture towards her mother whose impassive face is turned towards the sunlight.

"It's certainly caught your mother's attention there, hasn't it? Did you bring it in last night?"

"I did. It's actually an hour glass." Lisa feels bad correcting the lovely Glynis twice in swift succession, but Glynis only offers another sympathetically encouraging smile. "It has a faulty seal to the glass, we think. But it is one of mum's favourite possessions." Lisa looks down in surprise as her mother's hand squeezes her own – a gesture of gratitude?

Glynis gives another smiling nod. "Keep talking to your mum," she had said. "Hearing is the last thing to go. Tell her you love her, talk to her about your happiest memories. Make the most of this time together."

But Lisa is running out of happy memories. Lisa is instead horrifying herself with a wish that it could all be over soon, that this waiting for the inevitable could be shortened, wondering how much longer a worn-out body can survive after the medicines have been stopped, and food and drink are no longer necessities. The velvet plumpness of her mother's face had disappeared weeks ago; the figure in the bed was more unwrapped mummy than much-loved mum.

"I was saying to you earlier, wasn't I, Margot, what a lucky woman you are, so many beautiful grandchildren. And now this beautiful thing – is it a family heirloom?"

Lisa examines the ornament. It stands about two feet high, three elegant twisted spindles separate the highly burnished wooden discs that make up the top and base, sandwiching a long figure-of-eight glass, in which pale golden sand fills the top half, as if corked at the waist and waiting for release.

"We're not sure how old it is. It's just always been there, you know? Mum and Dad found it in the attic of their first home together, and Dad restored it. He reckoned it was Cuban mahogany – very rare and high-quality wood. So perhaps the sand is Cuban as well. It was broken then like it is today, and he couldn't find a fault in the glass, but there must be a seal to it somewhere, mustn't there? Anyway, he put it near the hearth in the hope the heat from the fire would fix it."

"And did it?"

"Yes - and it ruled our lives! Mum or Dad would turn it over and say: an hour of piano practice – or chores – or homework…"

Margot could add to that list, but she is drifting away to other memories, other times. She sees a tiny Victorian terrace, distempered walls, blackened with soot and damp; shabby picture rails and skirting boards. Then overlaid on that image, the same place but now bright with flowered wallpaper and the smell of new paint. The few bits of furniture are scrounged from family, friends and the local junk shops. The hour glass, shiningly restored but with its sand stubbornly sitting at the top of its prison, stands on the tiled hearth in the living room. The door swings open with a crash and Dan – Dan, in his wedding suit, young and dashing and full of life and love is carrying his beautiful, laughing and squealing bride ("Dan! Put me down! You fool!") through the door that leads straight into the small, square lounge where he deposits her on a battered settee and gives her the second long kiss of their married lives. In the silence there is a shooshing sound. The hour glass – was it the front door banging – or is the sand aware that a new life starts here? – has found a route for the blocked sand and it trickles through to the bottom, marking the first hour in their new home for Mr and Mrs Trent. "A blessing from the hourglass!" declares Dan. "I knew it would work, eventually."

And work it did, marking the hours of housework, cooking, and tasks both pleasant and unpleasant. "Give me an hour to get a start on it!" was Margot's catchphrase. Turn the hourglass over, make a start, and once a job's begun …

" – or football practice – or gardening …" Lisa smiles to suggest her list could continue for much longer.

"But it stopped again?"

The room goes quiet. Margot grips her daughter's hand. Lisa looks down at the chicken-skin claw, bruised and pin-pricked by cannulas. Her voice drops.

"Mum claimed it stopped again when Dad had his heart attack."

Margot remembers the sunshine dappling the kitchen floor as she baked Dan's favourite bread pudding to go into his lunchbox that week. Dan, two weeks from retiring; Dan, with his sunburnt bald spot, and his good-living paunch, which he blamed on Margot's cooking prowess; Dan, who lived for his growing family of kids and grandkids; Dan, who had dropped dead while mowing the lawn, his last words being a cry of "Margot!" as he fell. Only later, when she turned the hourglass over on return from the hospital – "dead on arrival – there was nothing they could do" – to will herself to spend an hour of phone calls to let people know, the sand had resisted a shake, and ignored hard taps to its bases, and refused to pour down into the lower cavity. And Margot had known it was another sign, the milestone that marked the start of her married life and the end.

"But still your mum loves it?"

"It's her favourite thing! It reminds her of Dad, she says, even more than his photos." Lisa gestures to the table where Dan at every stage of life grins out, always happy, always in sunshine, his family pride around him.

Glynis uses the opportunity to examine the photos, exclaiming at the cuteness of the children, the handsomeness of the males, the prettiness of the women, laughing at earlier fashions, lightening the atmosphere again before excusing herself. "You know where I am if you need me."

The sun is setting and a cool evening light blurs the shadows in the room.

Lisa's eyes have closed, although her hand still supports Margot's.

Margot's eyes have closed although her face is still turned towards the hourglass and the window.

No sound can be heard but the shallow breathing of two women in sleep, and then a shooshing sound, and then just the shallow breathing of one.

JARED RACE

Jared is a recent graduate of the University of Chichester's BA Creative Writing course. He enjoys writing fantasy and gothic stories, and spends his free time reading and wandering outdoors (often both at once).

The Straw-Man

BY JARED RACE

The car jolted over a bump in the road, and Marian's glasses slipped on her nose. By the time she had nudged them gently back into place, the farmhouse had come into view.

It was large. Larger than she had expected, and certainly larger than the internet ad had made out. Converted from a barn into a two-storey house, built from sturdy wooden timbers painted a peeling red, it towered up above the cornfields that surrounded it on all sides. It was almost a hundred metres from the road, accessed by a small dirt pathway that wound its way up through the maze of leaf and corn.

She pulled up to the side of the road as close to the pathway as she could get, noting a small gap cut into the field roughly the size of a car. After edging into the space, she clambered out and shook the kinks from her legs, wincing at how loud the slam of the car door sounded. The last email from the estate agent had mentioned a neighbour that would hand the keys over to her. A friendly face to introduce her to the area. But the road was empty, and silence pervaded over everything.

A small sign marked the entrance to the dirt road – '12 Twin Lake Road, New Haven, Connecticut'. She smiled briefly. New Haven was at least ten miles back the way she had come but in a country this size that was close enough for the house to fall within the town's limits. The distance was why she had chosen the place – away from the noise, and all the bad memories it conjured up.

She began the walk up the dirt path, and almost immediately the field seemed to envelop her. The corn rose to just above her head, but the first turn took her car completely out of sight, hidden behind a wall of yellow and green. The path was well-trodden but evidently unused for some time; small pockets of grass had begun to reclaim the scuffed ground.

She was almost halfway to the house when she turned a corner and let out a shriek.

She jammed a hand to her mouth, stifling the sound, and placed the other against her chest, in an attempt to bring her heartbeat under control. Silently cursing her own stupidity, she raised her eyes again to the figure before her, suspended a few feet off the ground by a long wooden pole stabbed deep into the ground. Its arms were stretched out to either side, slender limbs ending in sticks that stretched out like gnarled fingers. A faded brown coat covered its chest, and a wide-brim hat was tipped low over a face of coarse sackcloth, with crude stab-holes for eyes.

"Quite the sight, isn't he?"

Marian started once more but managed to keep from crying out this time. The speaker, a spindly grey-haired woman, stepped out from the next corner.

"Sorry for startling you," she apologised upon seeing Marian's face. "I heard you from the house, is all. Jane Redford – I live at number 11, a couple of miles from here. I assume you're the new owner?"

She seemed to barely pause between sentences, as though she was trying to force the words out as fast as she could. Marian managed a weak smile and nodded.

"Yes," she replied. "Sorry – I turned the corner and –"

"Mm," Jane nodded in understanding. She glanced up at the figure. "I call him the Straw-Man. He was put there by the previous owners. Odd choice, let me tell you. Very controversial." A shadow seemed to pass over her eyes. "Sometimes I wonder if that's the reason for everything that happened after."

Marian stared at her for a moment, waiting for an explanation, realising too late that Jane hadn't intended to give one. She turned her gaze away, but Jane had already seen it.

"Let's head on up to the house," she offered, gesturing a hand to Marian. "I'll tell you all about it as we go."

Marian nodded, her curiosity piqued. Jane cast another wary glance at the scarecrow before turning and leading her up the dirt path towards the farmhouse.

"You'll have moved here for the quiet, I suppose?" Jane asked as they trekked through the cornfield. "Traded up the old England for the new?"

Marian nodded. "Something like that." Fragments of memory bubbled to the surface: the riff of an Iron Maiden song, the faint smell of whisky.

"The Holmans were the same. Tony Holman – he was the father – he's the one that set up the Straw-Man back there." She wrinkled her nose. "I warned the man against it. No one puts up scarecrows around these parts. Bad luck, has been for decades. Course, Tony Holman wasn't from these parts."

"Why is it bad luck?" Marian asked. The farmhouse was coming into view once more ahead of them, and she felt a sudden urge to run for its shelter.

"Well," Jane said, inclining her head towards Marian's as they walked, "way back in the forties, this place was a hotbed for all manner of crazies and ritualistic-type folks. Not just your normal carny-fair freaks, I mean the *real* shit. Possessions and wicker men and voodoo, all that jazz." She cracked into a wide smile that showed gleaming white teeth and gestured her hands before her for emphasis. Marian wondered how long it had been since she had someone to talk to.

"Well, ever since then, folks around here have avoided scarecrows like the plague. Say that spirits still haunt these lands, and if you put up a scarecrow – well, that's a body just waiting for them." She finished with a smile and a shrug. "It's an old superstition, like I said."

They emerged from the cornfield into a wide circle, at the centre of which stood the farmhouse. Jane produced a set of keys from her dungaree pockets, prodded one into the door, and swung it open with a low creak.

"So what happened to them?" Marian asked as she followed the woman into the living room. What little furniture adorned the room was all hidden under dull white sheets, with a thick layer of dust over everything. "The Holmans, I mean."

"Ah, well," Jane murmured, pulling the sheet off of a wide sofa and gesturing for her to sit. "Hell of a tragedy, that was. Such a lovely family. No one really knows why it happened. One night, Tony just snapped. Killed his wife first – with a sickle, would you believe it. Anyway, he killed her, right through there in the kitchen. And then – well, then he went up to the kid's rooms." She shook her head, letting out a long sigh, and moved to lean back against a counter that looked through into the kitchen itself. "Hell of a tragedy. I saw them bring him out the next morning – kept screaming that he was innocent, even with the blood all down his front and his fingerprints on the sickle."

There was a long silence after she finished, and Marian realised that she had been staring. She dropped her eyes down to the floor. "Who else could have done it?"

Jane shot her a confused glance.

"If he said he was innocent, that is," Marian explained.

Jane frowned, and for a moment Marian thought she saw that same shadow dance across her eyes.

"Well –" she said, glancing out of a grimed window to where the corn-fields stood, a defensive wall around the property. "When they dragged him out, he kept saying – well, he said that the scarecrow killed them."

Marian's spine seemed to momentarily turn to ice, and she shuddered involuntarily. The movement wasn't lost on Jane, who gave her a wan smile.

"Don't you worry yourself about it," she said. "He was a troubled man, with a lot of problems. You ask me, I reckon he couldn't live with what he'd done. Rather blame a scarecrow than admit to killing his own family."

Marian nodded. "Yeah, I guess so." A thick silence settled over the room. Then Jane seemed to perk up and clapped her hands together.

"Anyhow," she said, "I should be getting back. I'll let you get used to the house – it's a simple layout, kitchen's just through that door there, with a larder running out to a back door. There's a spare room down here as well, and then upstairs there's the three bedrooms and a bathroom." She detached a thick iron key from her keyring and passed it to Marian. The movement took just a second too long, and the silence swept back into the room like flooding water. Jane noticed it too, and continued in a rush, "This unlocks the front door, the back-door key is in the lock. The estate manager – Lauren, was it? – she left the papers with me, I'll bring them over tomorrow. This sort of house can take a little getting used to, especially at this time of year, with the wind so strong an' all, so don't fret too much if you hear anything odd. I'm just a couple of miles up the road if you need anything."

With that she gave Marian a light pat on the back, before leaving through the front door, closing it lightly behind her.

* * *

The rest of the day seemed to pass quickly. The few belongings that she had been able to pack during her hasty departure had been assigned to places around the house, but they did little to remove the unease that she had for the place. She looked around the room, imagining a man holding a sickle, blood running like tears down the blade. Somehow the image was still comforting – a man was better than the alternative that Tony Holman had blamed.

Dispelling the vision, she set her laptop up in the master bedroom, on a bare desk that looked out through a window onto the expanse of cornfields below. The window adjacent to the bed had an even better view, opening out onto a field of pale yellow that stretched out towards the horizon, broken up only by the trees that lined the main road and a structure in the distance. She wondered if it was Jane's home.

Everything was lit in the warm orange glow of the dying sunset, and for a moment she could imagine being happy there, away from noise and crowds, fists and apologies. Then the sun passed below the rim of the horizon, and the light was extinguished from the room, as the land switched over from day to night like the flicking of a switch. A sudden draught made her shiver, and she turned to get ready for bed.

* * *

She sat bolt upright in bed, woken from a familiar nightmare into a room lit only by the faint moonlight seeping in from the windows. The dark expanse was blurred without her glasses, and she stretched an arm over to the bedside table, feeling about for the case. Her fingers came to rest on a smooth glass surface, and her phone blinked into life, reading '3:08'. As she searched she tried to work out what had woken her when it sounded again: a series of sharp, echoing taps.

Somebody was knocking at the front door.

Her blood turned to ice, and her arm froze over the bedside table. It brushed lightly over the solid shape of the key, and she relaxed slightly, remembering very clearly that she had locked it before going upstairs.

Her eyes flicked, almost without her willing it, to the window beside her bed. It was only a foot away from her. Through it, she knew, she'd have a wide view of the open space that lay between her house and the cornfield. And, most likely, whoever was knocking.

She got to her feet slowly, already trying to work out the reason that Jane could have had for visiting so late at night. A dark corner of her mind suggested a different visitor, and for a moment she imagined she could catch the scent of whisky on the air. Shaking her head to dismiss the ludicrous idea, she inched closer to the window. The moonlight was bright on the windowsill, the night beyond dark and foreboding. She took a shaky breath, bunched her hands into fists, and stepped up to the window.

Below her, standing motionless in the dark, was the Straw-Man.

Her mind scraped to a halt as she tried to reconcile the sight with anything resembling logic. The scarecrow's limbs were slim, arms ending in a tuft of hay and a spread of twig fingers. The wide hat cast shadows across a blank canvas face marked only by gaping black pits for eyes. The clothes were torn and frayed from years of exposure to the open air, leaking straw and filth in equal abandon, and around its neck, suspended from a rope tied into a hangman's noose, hung a sickle.

Marian tried to swallow, but the movement caught as if her body had forgotten how to function. As she stared down at the form below, eyes wide, the Straw-Man's hat tilted back. Its awful blank face looked up, and pitiless black eyes locked onto hers.

It was as if time suddenly jumped ahead. She jerked back from the window, the movement catching her so off guard that she fell against the bed. Her hands clawed the bedside table, scattering antidepressants and stray bits of paper until she found the torch. She staggered back to the window, the world beyond sparking into shades of yellow and orange as the beam cut an arc through the night.

The Straw-Man was gone. The world outside seemed entirely devoid of life. Miles of thin corn stems rustled back and forth in the wind, joining together in a strained whistle. Any one of the brushes of movement could have been the scarecrow, slipping away through the fields.

Marian stepped back, choking down a rasping sob, as the distant call of a crow sounded, a mocking laugh that echoed across the fields. She walked, as if in a trance, back to her bed. The blankets were cold to the touch, and she lay shivering, unable to draw her eyes from the window. Every sound made her twitch involuntarily. Every creak in the house made her glance at the door, expecting at any moment to see it swing open to show the shadowed straw shape beyond. She lay there in the darkness, alone with the nightmares that kept her from sleep.

* * *

The kettle let out a piercing trill. Marian started at the sound, eliciting a look of concern from Jane.

"I'm sure it was just a bad dream, dear," she said, pouring the water into the waiting cups.

"It wasn't a dream."

"Mm-hmm." The response was almost absent-minded as she shook the tea strainer slightly before lifting it out. "Do you take sugar?"

"No."

"Good girl. Now," Jane said, settling down into an armchair and handing Marian a steaming cup, an abashed smile on her face, "I must apologise for scaring you with such stories yesterday. It wasn't my intention, I assure you, it's just that company is rare around here and, well, I thought it best to give you an idea –"

"I didn't imagine it," Marian whispered, a tear building in her eye. She stared straight down at the steaming tea. Her gaze caught on a tiny black speck, floating on the surface, and she saw again that hollow, black stare.

"Well, whatever it was," Jane continued, "it's gone now. I have some old cameras lying around back at my place, I can bring it over if you'd like? Should keep any crazies away, at least."

"That'd be great. Thank you," Marian said, smiling gratefully at the kindly woman.

"It's no trouble. Here, sign these while I go pick them up," Jane said, passing over the sheaf of papers that had been the reason for her visit. "This area can be unnerving at first, but it really does grow on you. You made the right choice in coming here."

She gave Marian another warm smile and turned towards the door. As she left, a small strand of straw shook loose from her jacket, and drifted slowly downwards towards the ground.

KEVIN SLEIGHT

Kevin has had two short stories ('Taste' and 'An Eye For An Eye') recently published in a short story collection, *An Eclectic Mix, Volume 6*, after winning a competition run by Audio Arcadia.

He also recently won 1st prize with his short story: 'Just Another Half Empty Day In The Life Of Old Mr Grumpy' and two short plays ('Generation Game' and 'Cut!') in the Basingstoke Music and Arts Festival writing competition.

Born in Barry, South Wales, and a Maths graduate, he is retired now but has been a civil servant and an accountant. He is a life-long Stephen King fan.

Curtains

BY KEVIN SLEIGHT

*T*he bricks and mortar that had once been a vibrant suburban cinema were now just so many bricks held together by so much mortar. The light bulbs that had once emblazoned the night sky with the words 'Regency Grand' were no longer working. Never again would they throw their welcoming neon glow over snake-like queues of enthusiastic fans. The only visitors now were the graffiti artists who adorned the walls with an altogether different and far less inviting picture show.

Soon the bulldozers would raze this piece of the city's history to the ground, making way for a dozen or so sardine-like townhouses. No more waiting patiently in line for 'Gone with the Wind'. No more 'Elm Street' all-nighters. No more Wednesday afternoon Senior Citizen specials. Death-by-Multiplex had finally come to this Art-Deco shrine from an era long gone and hardly ever mourned.

Regan could have cried out loud. He'd grown up loving the movies. Still did for that matter. But an evening sitting next to kids stuffing themselves with bucket-sized tubs of popcorn had pretty much sounded the death knell on his love affair with the cinema.

The world had moved on.

Left this building behind.

Left him behind.

We're two of a kind, you and I, Regan thought, out of step with the times. Well to Hell with it, he didn't care.

For what little time remained, though, the cinema was his. An oasis in an urban desert. An inner sanctum from the mindless insanity that surrounded him.

Invisible in the darkness of the moonless night Regan entered the building unseen.

71

For what little time remained.

A home from home. And yet ... not a home from home. Rather, a home from what used to be home.

And a sanctuary. From a life gone to shit. A life torn apart at the seams.

Ten weeks ago, I found out my wife, Angela, was having an affair. She told me over tea and toast on a cold, wind-swept Saturday morning. My first reaction was to laugh. Our kids (one boy, one girl) are in their twenties, have left the proverbial nest and are struggling to make their own uncertain ways in the world. I'm fifty-five, my wife fifty, and, if we're honest, on both of us, age shows.

An affair. It was ridiculous.

I asked her why.

She said she needed to find herself. A way of putting it she probably incubated from an egg she'd found in the female pages of the Daily Mail.

Then she said it had nothing to do with me. Which was even more ridiculous. Of course, it had something to do with me! We'd been married for nigh on thirty years for God's sake.

I wanted to hit her. Not just a slap, but a clenched fist. I didn't. At the time I couldn't quite put my finger on what held me back. Later it came to me.

Revenge is a dish best served up cold.

I asked her if I knew the man. She said no. Then, somewhat gratuitously, she said he'd sold her her car, a Renault Clio. I did the maths. She'd bought the car about eighteen months ago. So not a quickie in the back seat. At least not just a quickie in the back seat.

I followed this no-brainer with the second obvious question. She couldn't get her answer out quick enough.

Yes, Michael, I want a divorce.

Fine. Just fine.

Not that it was fine. Not that it was fine at all.

And the other guy? Single. Convenient. At least this way I was the only one who got to suffer.

Only, as I said, revenge is a dish best served up cold.

The Regency (not so) Grand had been struggling to survive for at least a decade. Even converting its single screen to two screens (one up, one down) had been like pissing in the wind. The seats were uncomfortable. In the winter it was too cold, in the summer too hot. The choice of refreshments was limited. The staff were old. And they never got the (so-called) best films until they were well past their sell-by date.

Six months ago it finally closed. On its last night of opening, there were about fifty people there. I was one of them. They showed 'The Last Picture Show'. How the two brothers who owned the cinema managed to track down a copy of this '70s Bogdanovich classic, set in a dusty Texas town in the '50s where a rickety old cinema is about to close, I don't know. A nice ironic touch, I thought.

I went home that night and cried.

Angela had indulged me. As she had always indulged my love of the cinema. Lately, I guessed she could afford to. Getting me 'out of her hair' as she put it at least once a week must have been very, very convenient.

I'm not sure how the idea to break into the Regency came to me. I have to admit it was way off home base. Perhaps it was the rebel (without a cause) in me, I hear you ask? Causeless I certainly was. Rebel, on the other hand, I certainly wasn't.

I work for a firm of accountants in the tax department. It's good, steady employment and it pays well. If ever there was such a thing as the archetypical number-cruncher, I was it. If you were to pass me in the street, you'd do just that. Pass me in the street.

So, the worm turned.

I guess this means we all have our limits.

Press the right buttons, then stand back and watch the fireworks.

Breaking in was surprisingly easy. I waited until it was dark and parked around the corner. The front of the cinema abutted the street. There was a narrow lane to one side of the building that led to a small car park at the rear. A padlocked metal gate blocked off the lane and carried a 'Warning – Private Property – Trespassers will be Prosecuted' sign. It would have been no big deal to climb over the gate if I was younger and fitter or I had a ladder. I had no ladder because I had no intention of climbing the gate. Instead I turned my attention to the garden of the house next door. Getting into the garden over the not-so-high wall and through the garden's hedge – a hedge that like the Regency had seen better days – was, if not exactly child's play, at least doable, even for a middle-aged man like me. In the garden, I walked past the gate and then climbed back out again through the hedge and over the wall.

In the rear car park, I headed for one of the two Fire Exit doors.

I slipped the rucksack I was carrying off my back, opened it and pulled out the Heath-Robinson-hook-shaped piece of metal I'd crafted in my garden-shed man-cave. Slipped it between the narrow gap in the middle of the no longer pristine double doors and over the push bar on the other side. Pulled down hard.

It was a trick I'd seen performed years ago one evening when I'd been caught short in the middle of 'A Clockwork Orange'. The Regency's downstairs toilets were at that time located in two 'emergency exit' corridors on either side of the (only) screen.

I still wonder how much the two young lads who got in for free that night enjoyed the movie.

Now, as then, the doors unlocked and swung open. I'd half expected the bar to be chained or otherwise fixed to prevent the doors from opening. Keep out the winos, the drug addicts and the homeless.

I was lucky. Management hadn't fully battened down all the hatches. Probably didn't care any more. At some point no doubt they'd take whatever money they could get and run. And in the meantime figured who would want to break in? After all, the YMCA and the Samaritans were warmer, and they fed you.

Either way, this was one old lady who wasn't playing hard to get.

Inside I closed the doors behind me.

Took out my heavy-duty torch. Switched it on.

Felt this strange sense of belonging flood through me.

That was the first time.

The projection room was empty. Presumably, the projectors had already been sold to another cinema. Or perhaps just scrapped. Who knows?

Everything was digital now, of course, although in my nostalgia I imagined the projectionist spooling a roll of celluloid film. Switching on the powerful beam of light. Peering through the small window at the thinly populated auditorium.

Lights! Camera!! Action!!!

Welcome to another world.

Downstairs I took my pick of the seats.

It was pitch black inside the cinema. If it hadn't been for my torch, I wouldn't have been able to see a thing. I'd tried some of the lights, but they weren't working. Either the electricity had been disconnected, or the central fuse box had been pulled. Caution warned me against messing about with the fuses in case I inadvertently lit up any part of the building that could be seen from the street.

I sat down in a seat that rocked backwards none too gently in response to the weight of my body. Waved my torch over the screen.

Imagined John Wayne on a horse.

The owners of the Regency Grand were two brothers by the name of Paul and Joe Chomsky. Rumour has it they came to Britain from what was then the Soviet Republic in the 1960s. If this was true, they had obviously chosen to anglicise their first names whilst retaining their Russian origins. Another and equally unproven rumour has it that there was a third sleeping partner who put up the money to buy the cinema from a rich local family at a time when cinema attendances were in decline. True or false, the Chomsky brothers were well known around these parts and, being what I'd describe as a pair of loveable old rogues, were reasonably well respected.

Of course, respect counted for nothing when the choice was between The Regency, the Multiplex, a DVD or Netflix and fish and chips.

Like an old hooker with ladders in her stockings and one too many perms in her hair the Regency just couldn't score any more.

Sad to see it happen.

Very sad.

Three weeks after the big revelation Angela moved out. And I guessed that as soon as her, no doubt soon to be appointed, solicitor got his teeth into me the family castle would inevitably have to be put on the market. Enjoy it while I could. She, in the meantime, had moved in with her new soul-mate.

His name is Nigel. He is, I'd say, at least ten years her junior. A toy-boy in other words.

I hated him already.

Following him home from work was stupid really. I just wanted to see where he lived. Where she was living.

I parked outside his flat, not caring if Angela was there or not. And not caring if either of them was looking at me through almost drawn curtains.

Maybe he'd call the police.

Was I committing a crime?

More likely they were getting hot and sweaty and didn't know I was freezing my butt off outside.

Revenge is a dish best served up cold.

If my life was a Hollywood movie, this is how the film might have ended.

We see the adulterous couple making love in a bedroom. Cut to the street outside where the jilted husband sits in his car devouring a Mac-Donald's beef burger, fries and a shake. Like I said, this is a Hollywood movie. And it's clear the film is set somewhere in America.

Taking his time, the husband finishes his meal.

This isn't the condemned man's last supper though. Far from it. More like the executioner's.

The camera shows us a close-up shot of the gun on the passenger seat. Wiping the grease from his hands with a napkin, jilted husband picks up the gun and slides it under the belt of his trousers so that it's hidden by the jacket he's wearing.

He gets out of the car. Walks over to the house where his wife and her lover are having a good time.

Rings the door-bell.

Cut back to the bedroom.

"Who the hell's that?" asks lover boy. Although hubby doesn't know it, his timing is just perfect. Coitus interruptus. We are getting to the climax of the film in more ways than one.

"They'll go away," wifey says, not really caring whether "they" go away or not.

All of a sudden husband has no time for messing around. He shoots the lock, and the front door flies open.

At this point, we'll cut to the chase...

We're in an abandoned cinema. The lights are on. It doesn't really matter why the cinema has been abandoned. And it doesn't matter why the lights are on. The cinema has been abandoned because it's part of the plot that was set up more than an hour ago. The lights are on because this scene wouldn't work so well in the dark. At least in the mind of the director, it wouldn't. It's hard to tell when you're making a movie if you're in *Psycho 6* territory or a new classic in the making.

Lover boy and wifey are bound and gagged.

Husband has that look on his face. You know, Jack Nicholson in *The Shining* with an axe. Or Norman with a knife. Unhinged. Maniacal. It's payback time.

At this point in the story, it'd be nice if there was a movie playing in the background. Perhaps husband was a projectionist before his life took a nose-dive. A collector of old classics.

What would he have chosen?

Barbara Stanwyck and Fred MacMurray in *Double Indemnity* would be a good choice. An insurance salesman is ensnared by a femme fatale in a plot to kill her husband. Sex. Murder. Betrayal. Money. It'd do. It'd do just fine.

At what point will the husband pull the trigger?

You pays your money, and you takes your choice.

Maybe he'll make them wait until the end of the film he's watching. Let them stew in their own juices, so to speak.

Maybe he'll get it over with quickly so he can sit back and just enjoy the movie. Remembering of course that he'll need to change the reels.

Who will he shoot first? The wife or the lover?

Who deserves to get it first? Who deserves to see the other's head blown clean off?

I'll leave you to join up the dots. Fill in the blanks.

Run the movie in your mind.

See the blood.

Feel the pain.

We decided to tell our children together. It was the civilised thing to do. Neither of us wanted them to be upset. In this day and age, divorce is no longer a social stigma. Both Angela and I are still good old Mum and Dad. Just like we'd always been.

From our mouths to their ears.

Be not concerned.

Afterwards, I didn't know which hurt me the most.

Having to tell them not to worry about their mother and their father.

Or seeing how easily they did just that.

I mean, cope with the inconvenience. Not give a shit.

I'm back where I belong.

No longer a home-from-home but a home from a rented one-bedroom flat, the other place now sold and the net proceeds chopped in half.

It's dark. Jet black. I've turned off my torch.

I'm alone. So very, very alone.

A lost soul in this empty cavernous space.

The Regency (not so) Grand.

How much longer would it be now? How much longer before the sleeping pills do their job? An hour? Thirty minutes? Less?

As the time slowly passes, I imagine two heads, one male, one female, with gaping exit wounds.

Hold this in freeze-frame as I sink slowly into oblivion.

Angela stood over the grave telling herself she should at least be capable of a tear or two for this somewhat sad man who had been her husband for most of her adult life.

And yet the predominant emotion she felt was anger.

He had no right to kill himself, no right at all.

Couldn't he simply have accepted that she no longer loved him? Had not loved him for a long time. Had wanted to tell him but been unable to do so.

Finally, she'd found the courage to face the truth.

And this was her reward?

Surrounded by her children, relatives and friends, not listening to the priest's words on life after death, all Angela could think of was the welcoming embrace of her lover Nigel who would be waiting for her once this necessary ritual was over and done with.

The note had been pinned to the inside of the windscreen of Michael Regan's car.
He'd left the car parked on the double yellow lines outside the Regency.
    The note read:

Angela, forgive me. I can't live without you.
I've ridden off into the sunset.
The curtain has fallen.
The house is empty.
Save for one avid fan alone in a front row seat.

JACK ARNHOLD

Jack is a journalist and English teacher who splits his time between Rio de Janeiro and Bognor Regis (not such a stark contrast if you think about it). He writes for *The Rio Times* and is the city's 'local' for *Lonely Planet*.

Writing fitfully since 2011, he has completed a novel – which was enthusiastically rejected by literary agents and publishers – and a handful of short stories.

He does Twitter (https://twitter.com/jackarnhold) badly and Instagram slightly less so (www.instagram.com/jack.arnhold) and maintains a website (https://unimaginable-heights.neocities.org/) with his girlfriend where he occasionally writes about the Kardashians, how to cook a perfect steak, and other matters of importance.

The Cloud

BY JACK ARNHOLD

Had there ever been a day of such splendour? A Sunday, what a perfect name.

'Sun Day!'

I hauled myself up onto the roof (with the necessary Herculean struggle) and, once standing erect, I placed my hands on my hips and admired the endless sea of rooftops. I was above it all: above the swarming crowds that move like jet streams, above the beady eyes of fatigue that greet me at every tube stop, above the mule-like women, the mouse-like men – all those who don't look at you as an interesting phenomenon.

This was the apex of summer perhaps; it was certainly one of the hottest and most glorious days of living memory, and not a cloud in the sky. Wait, no, there were a few flecks. But I knew that in my lucky lifetime, I had known of nothing like this. My memories and recollections, that scrap heap of glad moments, seemed all the duller and less keen when held up to the luminance of this unique day's sky. I said to myself, "This only happens once in a universe."

For weeks now I had been coming up here, sacrificing social engagements, familial ties, work drinks, etc. My body slowly bronzing with each thin layer of afternoon sunshine. Unclothed, I resembled a fine piece of wood-stained heirloom furniture, or an ancient fragment of glazed terracotta. My skin had a lustre and depth of colour that suggested permanence and duration. Standing there on my roof I was a tree or a totem. Behold this man, I thought, here is a monument to the sun's clemency, here is an homage to the deep, thick, ancient forests where my ancestors sheltered and felled and lived: here is a centrepiece of life.

I had never had friends up there. I had instead chosen to carve out my own private sanctuary, away from the eyes and the crowds and the sirens. When I went to work, I was careful to button up my shirt all the way, so that no-one could see what lay beneath. My face was a given, but that in itself, I knew, was quite unremarkable. I had a face in the same way that people have palms. It was nondescript, except maybe, I thought as I had lain awake some nights, to some enchanted person. Just like there are palm readers who find these banal pads of flesh so poetic and full of mystery, there might be someone out there who would find the same intrigue, subtly laced in my mediocre visage. But this is beside the point.

When I think about that Sunday, I can still hear a vague sound of happy catcalls and laughter. I can still sense, in all directions, a soft and distinct hum of leisure. I can taste the azure blue of the sky, the subtle and dusty fumes from the streets below, and that moist verdure of a distant roof garden.

Where there was at first a touch of cloud in the sky, the sun increased in intensity and burned away much of it, until there was nothing but blue sky and white heat. The families and couples and sets of friends one by one left their roofs as the mercury continued to climb. No-one was around. I glanced from roof to desolate roof, each one baked and black and shimmering in the sultry heat. They looked like pools of tar, waiting to swallow a hapless dinosaur.

The afternoon waned, and a pleasant and constant breeze was blowing across the empty skyline, and I felt the need to fully make the most of this precious meeting between me and the sky and the sun. I did what I'd always wished to do when up there, what I'd always suspected others of doing in my absence. I pulled down my shorts, then my damp grey underpants, tossed them to one side and stretched out my fully naked body on the lounger. I was in my birthday suit. I was the father of Adam. I was a pagan hero. And in my mind, I was making love to the sun.

I had often fantasised about this moment, how it would feel, how it would be. The loftiness was quite sublime. My body was smooth and glistening. I looked down from my chest to my stomach and lower, and I could see those arbitrary demarcation lines that signified 'parts of the corpus fit for view', and 'parts that must remain unseen!' The contrast was quite striking, but not offensive; my pubic region resembled a snow-covered valley surrounded by a vast ochre desert, my penis lay there like a bald polar bear, lolling in the blissfully unseasonal weather.

I looked out, up into the light blue haze and felt a connection with not just the sky and the earth, but with the arching embrace of the universe. I had a beautiful realisation that there was nothing now in front of me, for most likely a few thousand miles, if not millions. Nothing was weighing me down but air.

Time passed without notice. I remember seeing a few clouds in the distant west, huddled together. I thought nothing of them. The roofs were still deserted, and I was becoming more and more used to this glorious state of undress, this Adamite afternoon.

I don't know why exactly, but I began to fill with the most ecstatic joy. As I rose, I felt like a plant, reaching up to the sun, the creator. I felt like the first plant on earth. I felt the very essence of life surge through my body. My pleasure was intense and tectonic. However, what was once a clear and blue sky, to my unknowing, was becoming slightly cloudy. The clouds assembled, under the sun, and began to drift with purpose in my direction. One by one, each momentarily cloaked my exposure to the universe. Then a most curious thing happened. One of the clouds stopped directly above me. I knew this because the shadow – the brief touch of cold that caressed me with each passing cloud – lingered.

I stopped dancing. I say dancing, it was more of a Dionysian invocation, a love song to the universe. I looked up at the cloud, and it hurried on, following the rest of the herd, as they rolled away like a lost pack of migratory continents. But once I had stopped, something within me tightened. I couldn't enjoy the day anymore. I began to question myself, my eyes, my judgement, my sanity. I was sure I had seen that cloud pause, take note of my joy, and then move on. A light wind had risen, and soon I had buttoned up my shirt, pulled up my pants and shorts and wearily descended from my heights.

Needless to say, I had slept unsoundly and went into work in my usual fog of apathy. I don't want to go into the humdrum details of what happened the next day, as I find descriptions of work life so myopically voyeuristic and needlessly judgemental. Man has to work. I doubt whether the hunter-gatherers found their work particularly 'rewarding' or 'meaningful', but if they did well at the office, it meant they could eat that night, and perhaps daub the cave wall with their painted fingers

My office is small but well air-conditioned. I know my colleagues by first name, my bosses by first and last name, and usually enter the office last or second to last, depending on whether *he* has been staying with his parents again. He stays there occasionally to 'look after' them, though he's the sort of forty-year-old child that, if it were socially acceptable, would happily wear a bib to meals. He probably still breast-feeds, but that's entirely beside the point. He was early, and I was the last into the office.

I shuffled in, acknowledging the usual sights and sounds of mundanity. The posters, birthday cards, reminders, mugs of lukewarm tea, were all where they were meant to be. The sound was a familiar one, the sound of multiple fingers caressing keyboards. It always gives me the creeps and reminds me of some farm for giant scuttling insects. I saw the rolls of fat and the pasty skin that resembled uncooked dough. I sat down in my chair and started up my computer terminal. I logged on, and to my surprise found an internal email addressed to me. It had been carbon-copied to everyone in the office but was specifically addressed to me. It read 'Nice Dancing, Dude' and had no other text, only a small video of some swarthy man feverishly dancing on a rooftop. 'Rooftop Mentalist' one comment read (there were hundreds), 'Funniest Video', etc. Most were moronic and poorly spelled affairs; the video had over four million views, and as I looked further, there were videos of people watching the video, there were videos of people re-enacting the video, there were videos of the video with added music or jarring cuts and loops of the footage.

Everywhere I looked on the screen, and in the office, there was only that recurring image of the pulsating, dancing, naked man. The office erupted in a weak and unsteady unison of laughter. I realised that I had unwittingly pollinated the imagination of this dim planet. None of my colleagues turned around or addressed me by sight or by name. One of them vocally reiterated the subject line, 'Nice Dancing, Dude!' and everyone laughed again, as nervous and unsure as the first time. I felt saddened by this, saddened and angry. I looked around the office again, but no-one would meet my gaze. I looked around at all these pale and shapeless men and women and felt enormous pity. They had touched my vintage oak, they had visited my hideout in the heavens, they had danced with me under the mercy of the warming sun, and yet they had done none of these things.

I left work that day with the same uncanny fug polluting my thoughts and intentions. I realised I had been betrayed by that curious cloud. I felt that I too was becoming more and more cloud-like. And that part of my essence had dissipated and was dissipating with each carbon copy of myself, playing over and over again in the unconscious swarm of the internet.

I don't remember too much about what happened next. I remember waking up slumped on my toilet, in the dark and covered in sweat, looking up from the bowl and seeing the cloud crouched in the top corner of the bathroom, then watching it as it slithered down and silently crept out under the door. I remember I was furious that I hadn't seen the signs, all over the underground: 'The Cloud is coming', 'Get a Cloud of your very own'. I remember seeing that advert with a man walking a cloud on a leash. Bits of me were falling apart, every time I coughed I heard a piece of life go. I was becoming more and more elemental in my nature. Some people have the misfortune of being born invisible, others learn to become invisible, but I was marching boldly against a headwind that was stripping me of myself, atom by atom.

A few days later, now I'm recounting this from what I've heard – not what I did – there was another sighting of that swarthy man on the roof. The day was raining, and the sky was swollen with clouds. Some people said that they saw a man on my roof, dancing more feverishly this time. He was dancing and dancing and, with an old rifle, was shooting up into the sky and laughing ferociously. Others only saw the laughing man, but said that he was naked, others say that they saw him disappear from the roof, others that they saw a man lying on the pavement and that he was carried away by ambulance or some other flashing car. I don't know which one is true. I don't care. From what I've heard, from what I've seen, it was beautiful.

MARALYN GREEN

Maralyn is a published non-fiction writer, and now also enjoys writing fiction stories of all types and lengths. She is a valued member of the Bognor Regis Write Club and a fellow judge.

Changes Of Heart

BY MARALYN GREEN

The bullet slammed into his chest, jerking him back as his feet skittered over the sodden mud. At first no pain, just shock. Numb shock, rendering the bloody bombardment around him meaningless. 'Onward!' yelled his mind. 'Forward!' reverberated his orders. On and on, step by slow step in the sludge, the quagmire of stinking sludge mired with bones and bodies. Without warning, blistering heat burned along his shattered nerves. Had he been hit a second time? The pain ricocheted violently within him as he stumbled, half-swaying, into 'No Man's Land'. He could not last. A few yards more and the burden of rifle, bayonet, grenades and ammunition dragged his trembling knees ever nearer to that black ooze underfoot. Almost as he succumbed, a massive blast from a nearby artillery shell hurled his body into the putrid graveyard of a nearby crater. His pack and uniform, nearly torn off in the immediate shockwave, were no cushion as he landed heavily on his back. In a whispered breath came a faint appeal "Mother! Millie!" before all conscious thought receded. He lay still and senseless, his face clear of the Flanders mud, his body unseen by enemy snipers.

The roar of battle continued around and over him all day, as British soldiers tried to storm the German front line. Futile gestures and wasted lives, vainly driven in desperate attempts to break the mud-drenched stalemate of trench warfare. As darkness fell, cold dampness seeped into his senses and brought Albert back to semi-consciousness. When he could no longer block out the continued gunfire, thundering explosions and the human screams of battle, with the occasional fainter sounds of voices, soldiers' voices shouting obscenities across the fields from the so-called safety of their foul burrows, Albert opened his eyes.

Uncomprehending at first as the blackness of night filled his vision, he closed his eyes, shut out the world and fought to believe this horror was but a dream. Yet dreams were not cold, not painful, nor ever this deafening. He dreaded the knowledge that swept over him. No, he didn't want to accept that he was still in the hell hole of Ypres. "Millie, Millie …" Escape had not come as yet, but he felt its nearness, deep inside him and he knew there was not too long to wait. He could not stir any part of his body. Only his eyes opened up to the darkness above, where faint starlight strained against the intermittent flash of mortars. Only his memories stirred within him.

"Millie, sweet Millie. You couldn't know what you sent me to. Trenches reeking like cesspits, and mud, never-ending mud, with endless mindless shelling, and for what, a few inches of a farmer's field. Living on top of men I'd never met, and probably would never want to in another life, but then watching them blown to bits. Blown to bits if they were lucky, with bits blown off if they're not so lucky. Oh Millie, remember how you thought I'd return the conquering hero and you'd cheer, cheer like mad and wave a flag for me as we marched home. 'I'll be so proud of you, so proud,' you said gently, looking as though you saw me already in that role. And man that I am, I gazed at your adorable face, watched your lips part as you spoke, heard the sweet promise in your voice, and so longed to be that hero for you."

Albert was engulfed with helpless emotions, a longing for all that had been wiped so abruptly from his future, for all that could now never be. He remembered last year, and he remembered Millie. Lazily strolling down Richmond Hill, his summer blazer unbuttoned and straw boater in hand, he had seen a mass of auburn hair in front of him, his attention caught by a few curls escaping their pins, softly swinging and shining in the early autumn sunlight as it glinted through the trees. For Albert her hair flamed, and so did he. He couldn't take his eyes from her curls, from her slender back, from her at all. He felt breathless, even running a finger round his stiff collar to gulp for air. How idiotic, he thought, to fall for a girl, face unseen, just on account of her beautiful hair. Yet Albert had known in that moment, no matter what, he had to meet this young Titian-haired lass.

His pace quickened for he must see her or quit this idiotic pursuit. Yet instinctively he knew there would be no quitting. In some part of himself, the decision had already been taken. Drawing ever closer, he had followed her silently, wondering how to introduce himself. Then fortuitously, with only a few steps between them, she had tripped lightly on some unevenness beneath her feet. She would have corrected this without help, but Albert saw his chance and firmly leapt forward and took hold of her arm, enquiring, as he did, if she was alright. Millie, who had been oblivious to her pursuer, was somewhat taken aback by this sudden and unwelcome seizure of her person. She looked over her shoulder in confusion, glancing up at the tall stranger and attempting to shake herself free. In doing so, she dropped the letters she had been carrying to post, and lifting her long skirts and petticoats, bent down to pick them up.

Albert, for his part, had been entranced by the blue-grey eyes and freckled nose momentarily turned towards him, his breath caught and so he was slower to respond. Yet with his hand still firmly on Millie's arm, he too eventually found he had to bend down. The time delay between their two actions meant that Millie was starting to stand up again, as Albert's head descended, and the inevitable connection was made with a glancing blow on Albert's nose.

Ah, recalled Albert, had that been the point of no return? There could I have apologised, or accepted her delicate apologies, turned away and indeed turned off the path of death? But no, never had such thoughts entered Albert's mind. At the time, through his smarting eyes, above his throbbing nose, he'd seen her face come close to peer at his, with tiny frown lines forming between her brows. His heart had leapt with the nearness of her and he'd known that this was but a beginning for him. She'd looked around and gestured towards a shaded bench nearby, saying, "Do please sit down for a while. I really am so very sorry. Oh, what have I done? I do hope I have not broken anything … I mean you have not broken anything. I mean … oh dear, are you hurting very badly?" Albert, with a hand over his nose, had attempted to say, "Please don't worry yourself, I'll be fine," but his voice had sounded thick as though with cold. He'd smiled to reassure her and was charmed by the shy smile in return that spread from her lips up into her eyes. He'd found himself in a difficult position as he wanted to present the demeanour of one still hurting whilst manfully trying to maintain an outward appearance of calm. He was aware that it was a shameful pretence as the pain was fast subsiding, but he didn't want her to leave.

She was Millie, and she'd promised a rather persuasive Albert that she would meet him again to make sure he was recovered. That next time, as they wandered side by side over Richmond Bridge watching pleasure boats on the river below, they laughed about their clumsy introduction, and Millie could see that the bruising Albert had sustained was minimal. Albert admitted his subterfuge and they laughed some more, and it was infectious, and so they began, in gentle humour, to know each other.

Albert remembered how their relationship had deepened against an increase of international tension in the world beyond them. If there were those who predicted war, it never troubled Albert, for he was not, what is termed, 'able-bodied'. A good physical specimen, a couple of inches over six foot and broad-shouldered, but childhood polio had left him with a slight limp, and inheritance had not bestowed him with excellent sight. His mother was apt to say, "My Albert will always support his country, but his battle will be fought on the home front."

As the descent to war became inevitable, the girls of Millie's acquaintance, fired up by national propaganda, urged their brothers and suitors to volunteer. Millie tried to persuade Albert that he should take up arms, but Albert pointed out the obvious – he wasn't suitable material. Millie wouldn't, couldn't, leave it at that; for all the young men in her circle were going to be officers or soldiers.

"Millie, oh Millie," thought Albert. "Why did you try to send me away? Was it for me or for you? Would your pride have been hurt if I had stayed at home? Perhaps you couldn't have borne to be the only girl not writing or knitting for her soldier. So is it for that I have to lie here in a field, far from home, just for your bloody pride? Hell, if I hadn't listened to you, woman, been cajoled by your smile, your words, or been intoxicated by the nearness of you, I'd be safe today. God, how I despise those wheedling ways, your cunning smiles designed to get just what you wanted – what about me, what did I get? Millie, I should have turned away from you. I should have heeded my mother. Mother, you were right, so right."

If Albert could have cried loudly and wildly for what he had lost, he would have done so. As it was his tears swept down through ingrained grime and lengthening stubble, but there was no sound. Back at home, his mother had slumped in her chair, aghast to hear that he was considering Millie's suggestion of trying to volunteer. She had begged him, as her only son, not to do so. Hadn't he every excuse not to be so foolish, and finally, well, they wouldn't take him anyway, would they? But there was an awful fear in both that in a desperate situation he might well be taken for King and country. Albert, when apart from Millie, could see his life more clearly and thought better of such bravado, but he still feared Millie and her determination.

Fatefully, one weekend, at a house party with friends, Millie whispered, whilst leaning close against him, so that he could feel the very curves of her body and inhale her faint musky scent, which so aroused him, "I'd be so proud of you, Albert." Then brushing her lips softly against the lobe of his ear, she murmured again, "So proud, Albert." He half closed his eyes as his body responded to her presence, he felt confused, and Millie, sensing victory, entreated, "You will go, won't you, Albert?" He wanted to say 'Yes' to her, he wanted her, oh yes he did, and so he let himself surrender to his senses, nodding his head with the knowledge somewhere in the back of his mind that his acquiescence was not truly binding. But Millie had other ideas. Quickly calling their friends to listen, she announced, "Albert is going to volunteer!" There was some surprise, but mostly a lot of backslapping and handshaking from the men, and undisguised looks of admiration from the women. Albert found himself trapped when the inevitable followed and he volunteered the next day. His male pride minimised his physical problems and he was somehow accepted.

"Bloody pride!" thought Albert. "That's why I'm here. Your pride and mine, Millie. I should have left you, Millie, what use am I to you or you to me now? My dear God, Millie, won't you just look so good in black! Oh yes, you'll cry in your black. Tears will stream down your face and you'll be proud of the man who gave his life for his country. Proud for what? This death that means nothing. I will die because of you, Millie, only because of you. And what have you done, what have you suffered, what have you sacrificed? Nothing. Not a single thing. And me, what is left of me? Will I look good with the maggots eating away at my face, with the skin slowly stripped away from my bones? Oh, how mad was I to have ever listened to you. You and your selfish ways. Always thinking about how you will look, what people will think of you. Yes, I wish with all my heart that I had never met you, Millie. I wish I'd never seen your bright hair, never stopped you, never laughed with you, never been taken in by your wheedling words. What a fool I was, what a stupid fool! If only I had just turned and walked away, far, far away from you."

Faint wisps of a red dawning flowed across the sky, but for Albert, the beauty of nature no longer had any meaning. He was consumed by his thoughts and racked with an anger more powerful than any he had ever known.

"'Ere, Bill, over 'ere, here's another unlucky bugger." Two British soldiers wriggled and slid their way into the crater and did a brief check of Albert. "Blimey, he's alive, better get him back to the Palace." Dragging down a blood-stained stretcher, still damp from its last wretched occupant, they accidentally bumped Albert with one of the wooden poles. Albert, finding his voice at last, could only croak, "Leave me ... I'm gone."

Laughter erupted above him, "Love a duck, a talking corpse." The laughter was quickly squashed as the ground rocked again from more blasts and his wise-cracking rescuers fell as flat as Albert lay. Nothing daunted, the repartee soon continued much closer to Albert's ear. "Look, mate, you ain't gone yet. Got a bit more time left in you, if I know anything about it, but I'll do you a deal ... OK?" A reply was expected, but this time nothing came from Albert's ashen lips. Not bothered at all, the Cockney voice soon pressed on, "Well, see here, if you don't make the journey back, we'll promise to dig you a much better 'ole than this one out 'ere." And the two soldiers chuckled some more at what must have been a well-worn joke ... but still a good'un.

The trench humour was lost on Albert. Anger and pain were eating their way down into the very sinews, tissues and cells of his being. He had all but given up when sturdy hands grabbed his shoulders and ankles, jarring his ruptured chest and thrusting him into a world of heightened agony. Hauled onto the canvas stretcher, his tortured body shrieked out as they set off at a merciless pace, pushing him down and pulling him up, in and out of one crater after another, with never a care for the detritus of war that he was being bumped across. Albert was screaming "Stop!" as he fainted, only to be jolted back into unwilling, painful consciousness all too soon.

At what point they slid him back over the front line, he was far beyond caring. Not even when the canvas was lifted off the ground and carried into the medical area, at a safer distance from the line of fire, did he register much, apart from a relief of sorts. "You'll be alright 'ere at the Palace, mate," said his muddied would-be saviour, "Give 'im a bit of time. The Doc, I mean. He actually does save quite a few."

The Palace turned out to be a windowless, concrete bunker, providing slightly more shelter than a trench, but men were still sardined inside on wooden trestle tables. Around them, the air was clogged with a fetid mix of carbolic lotion and vomit, yet to Albert it mattered little where his last breath was to be taken, as no part of this bloody bungled confrontation was choice in that regard. He was readying himself to leave the pain and depart from this world, when he became conscious of gentle fingers probing his chest. Mastering his suffering, he managed to gasp, "Leave me, I know I'm dying."

The doctor, who had been doing a careful examination of Albert, grinned briefly and then said, "Look, you might be feeling pretty grim, but it really doesn't seem to be that bad. Bit of concussion, nasty bullet wound, but not fatal, missed your vital parts ... I'd say we patch you up here, stem the bleeding, then some surgery plus convalescence and you'll do fine. Though I wouldn't know if you'll be back with us after, but that's no disaster, is it?"

Albert stared at the doctor. Death had suddenly receded into the distance, but so quickly had it cleared away that his battered brain could not cope with the vacuum left behind. He was in shock again. He had to slowly savour the words, 'you'll do fine'. He needed to relive the telling of them and also treasure the meaning of them. Was that really 'fine' as in living, going back home, walking, seeing his mother, his dear mother, lifting her up in his arms and hugging her once again? 'Fine' as in daring to think of a future now, a future that had all but disappeared, yet a future already filling up with more and more possibilities.

'Fine' as in seeing Millie again. Millie, beautiful, shining-haired, Millie.

"Millie" he croaked, "get out your flag, I'm coming home. Millie, oh Millie, my sweet love, I'm coming home to you."

PATRICIA FEINBERG STONER

Patricia is a former journalist, advertising copywriter and publicist. For four years she and her husband were accidental expatriates in the Languedoc, southern France, for reasons which seemed good at the time.

Her first book, *Paw Prints in the Butter*, is a collection of comic verse about cats, and is sold in aid of a local animal charity. Her second, *At Home in the Pays d'Oc*, is a humorous account of her adventures in France.

Following a second foray into the world of comic verse (*The Little Book of Rude Limericks*), in the autumn of 2018 Patricia published *Tales from the Pays d'Oc*, which revisits the locales of *At Home in the Pays d'Oc* in a collection of 21 humorous short stories. In its pages you will discover what Matthieu was doing in the olive tree, who stole the Indian prawn and who rescued two stranded Americans at Armageddon Falls.

Patricia welcomes visitors to her Facebook page, 'Paw Prints in the Butter', and to her blog: www.paw-prints-in-the-butter.com. You may occasionally find her on Twitter: @perdisma.

Stick in the Mud

BY PATRICIA FEINBERG STONER

"Come on, Mary. Don't be such a stick in the mud. It'll be an adventure." George did his best impression of a walrus, peering up at her over his abundant moustache. "Jamie's in the States now, and Meg's off travelling as soon as she finishes uni. Don't we deserve a new start, too?"

Mary regarded her husband with some distaste. The years had not been kind to George: never a big man, he had shrunk with age. His once-firm cheeks had fallen into pendulous jowls, the hair on his head stood out in sparse tufts, and his stomach cascaded over the belt of his tattered jeans. Mary had always prided herself on 'keeping up'. She went to Slimming World every week, dutifully ate her five a day and had her hair styled once a month at Clarice's in Ladbroke Grove.

"Why on earth would we want to up sticks and go and live by the seaside? The only person we knew in Rustington was your mum. Now the old witch has finally gone to ... wherever, I thought we'd be shot of the place for good."

George was not to be deterred. "You know I've always fancied getting out of London one day. Haven't you had enough of the noise and the dirt, not to mention it taking hours to get anywhere because of the traffic? Now we've got Mum's house, it's a God-given opportunity. Besides," George played his trump card, "Barney would love the garden."

Barney had been lying, paws crossed, by the front door. He was bored, wondering if his humans would ever stop talking and take him for a walk, the best part of his day. Hearing his name, he looked up and woofed, tail thumping wildly. "Now?" said his odd-coloured eyes. "Is it time?"

"Not long, old boy," said George. He clicked his fingers and Barney trotted over for a scratch behind the ears. "You tell your mum," George went on, "that if we went to live in Sussex you'd have a lovely big garden to play in and a beach to run on every day."

Mary sighed. George usually managed to get his own way. She weighed it up. A Londoner born and bred, she loved the capital city: the noise, the people, the theatres and galleries, the West End cafes and the little hidden gems of restaurants tucked away in side streets. She loved their top-floor flat in West Hampstead. She loved the gracious Art Deco lines of the building; they had decorated their flat to reflect the period.

Her husband might have a point, though, she conceded. Buildings and people get older. Their old bird-cage lift, picturesque though it was, was more often out of order these days than working, and trudging up four flights with the shopping was getting more tiresome every week. Soon, Mary knew, the residents of the block would be facing yet another bill for renovation, and even divided among thirty-four flats it would still be substantial. Moving to a warm, fully furnished house with a large garden might not be such a bad thing after all. At least Rustington was within striking distance of the theatres of both London and Chichester.

The move went smoothly. George, of course, settled in right away, and for two or three months Mary was happily occupied, redecorating, putting the garden to rights and getting to know the area. Came the day, as she knew it would, when she looked up and thought, "What next?"

She tried the WI and was not impressed. "I can't sing, and I can't make jam and all the women do is talk about their grandchildren," she complained to the newspaper that hid her husband's face.

A friendly neighbour suggested the U3A. At first, Mary was horrified. Spend afternoons cackling with a load of old biddies? Not her! She was young – well, young-ish – and vital; no way was she ready for a kaffee-*klatsch*. "No," her neighbour insisted, "it's not like that at all. You have no idea how many different groups there are. You are bound to find something interesting."

Working her way through the directory lent by the helpful neighbour, Mary was indeed surprised and decided to put a toe in the water. She tried the creative writing group first, but the leader, a thin, bossy woman, told her off for talking too much and criticised her use of adjectives. She sampled the ramblers' group, but the large woman with an opinion on everything soon put her off. Spanish conversation looked promising, but although there was plenty of conversation going on it was mostly in English, despite the very best efforts of the group's leader.

What to do? Mary was on the point of giving up when one more group caught her eye. It was called 'Out and About', and promised to take its members to some interesting places. There was a meet and greet once a month at the Arun View in Littlehampton; she'd go along and see what it was all about.

She walked diffidently into the bar, rather daunted by the group of chattering people who all seemed to know each other rather well. Then the leader rose to welcome her. Mary gasped, then hastily suppressed a giggle. He was such a cliché! A couple of years younger than her, she reckoned, tall with rugged good looks and blue eyes flashing beneath midnight-dark brows. He looked like something out of a story in a woman's magazine. And the way he looked at her! Irrationally, she was suddenly conscious of her tired Marks & Spencer bra, her non-matching knickers.

"I'm Jake," he purred, "and you must be Mary." She resisted the urge to say, "You must be joking," settling for a simple, "Yes, I am." She was soon welcomed into the group, which seemed to consist of people around her own age, but who were still 'making the effort', as she called it. The men were in trousers or well-cut jeans with not a paunch to be seen. The women wore casual dresses or what looked like designer jeans, with colourful tops – some a little lower cut than Mary would have dared.

Tuesdays took on a new charm for Mary. All week she looked forward eagerly to meeting her new friends and going to new places. There was a backstage tour of the Chichester Festival Theatre, a visit to Canine Partners, a summer trip to Benbow Pond for a picnic. The group seemed very close, rather touchy-feely, with lots of shared jokes and lingering glances. Mary enjoyed the intimacy, but began to wonder ... She wasn't totally surprised, therefore, when about six months after she had joined the group the handsome Jake took her to one side. "Some of us also meet up in the evenings," he confided. "It's a rather, er, special gathering, for couples who want to do something a bit more adventurous. Do you think your husband might like to come along?"

Mary stared at him blankly for a moment, then the penny dropped. "You mean it's ..."

"Sshh." Jake put a finger on her lips, causing her to quiver in unexpected places. "Have a think about it and let me know."

Mary was busy over the following couple of weeks. She ventured into Angel White in Littlehampton and made an appointment to have her hair styled and highlighted. Greatly daring, she signed up for a bikini wax as well. On the pretext of a U3A outing, she travelled to Brighton and visited *Victoria's Secret*, hiding the pink and white carrier bag inside a plastic one from Tesco. Then she made the phone call.

"Jake?" She tried to suppress the tremor in her voice. "I was wondering ... well, you did suggest my husband and I might come to an evening meeting?"

"Mary! I'm so glad you called. As a matter of fact, we're having a gathering at my house on Saturday week. Do come along."

Now there was just the matter of George. As far as he was concerned, Saturday nights were for sitting in front of the television with a takeaway and *Britain's Got Talent*. Mary pondered the best way to persuade him to go out.

"You know that group I've been going to? 'Out and About'?" she began. "Well, they're having a little party next Saturday evening, and they've invited me along."

"That's nice, dear."

"No, well, actually they've invited *us* along. The invitation said, 'other halves welcome'. I thought you might enjoy it for a change."

"No chance," George said firmly. "I'm not about to spend my Saturday evening with a load of old farts, thank you very much."

"It's not like that," she protested. "They are very interesting people." Crossing her fingers behind her back, she went on: "Jake, the leader, has a huge model train set-up. I'm sure he'll show it to you, and you can have a good old natter about 'O' gauges or whatever. And his wife's an amazing cook. Jake once brought in some paella she'd made, and it was heavenly. Do let's go along, just this once."

Appealing to his stomach had the desired effect; George allowed himself to be persuaded.

Mary had a new dress for the occasion, showing a little more of her cleavage than usual. "You look nice, dear," said George, vaguely. "Have you done something to your hair?"

Jake lived in a sprawling three-storey house on the outskirts of Littlehampton. Walking into his warm, softly lit living room, Mary was pleased she had made her preparations: the group was even more resplendent than usual.

"Welcome," said Jake, handing her a glass of prosecco.

George's eyes were immediately drawn to the platter of tapas on a low coffee table, and it was several minutes before he noticed the cut-crystal bowl beside it.

"There's a bowl of key rings over there, what's that all about?" he asked his wife.

"Don't worry about it, dear, just give me the car keys."

He handed them over and watched, with dawning comprehension, as Mary casually tossed them into the bowl.'

"Mary!" her husband spluttered. "Mary, this is …"

Mary shushed him. "Come on, George. Don't be such a stick in the mud. It'll be an adventure."

Mother Love

BY JULIA MACFARLANE

The porch light snapped on as Lydia pulled her car into the drive and switched off the engine. Jake stroked her cheek and said, "I hope this weekend goes OK."

"We'll be fine. I'm looking forward to it." Lydia leant across to kiss him but he pulled away when the dormer bungalow's front door opened. A woman left the house and moved towards the car.

"You're late!" she began.

Jake held up his palms as he stepped out of the car. "You know what the traffic's like on a Friday evening. Mum, may I introduce Lydia to you?"

Lydia was struggling out of the driver's side. "And it was my fault, too, Mrs Bellamy. I couldn't escape from work as early as I would have liked."

"Well, you could have called. Dinner might have been ruined." This was addressed to Jake, rather than Lydia.

"Now, now, Rita, let the young ones into the house before you start scolding them." Mr Bellamy, framed in the doorway of the porch, was a plump man in a rugby shirt, faded jeans and slippers. He stepped out and opened his arms to Lydia. "So you're Jake's new squeeze? Welcome to our humble abode; we've been hearing a lot about you the past few months."

Lydia raised her eyebrows at Jake with a grin as she mouthed "New squeeze?" then allowed herself to be folded into the older man's arms. She turned to Mrs Bellamy for a matching hug and realised just in time that she was being offered a handshake.

"Please call me Rita. Would you like to freshen up while I start putting the food onto the table? Jake will show you the way."

100

Jake removed their holdalls from the boot, and the younger couple followed the elder into the house.

"She seems nice," Lydia laughed into Jake's ear.

"I did warn you." He whispered back.

"Your dad's OK."

"One hug and you're putty in his hands. You're such a tart." He gave her a quick kiss on the mouth.

"Jake," His mother's voice parted them. "Could you show Lydia up to the guest room? You'll be sleeping in the drawing room, I'm afraid."

"The drawing room?" Lydia followed Jake up the stairs. "Is that next to the morning room, m'lord?"

"Behave yourself. It's never been called that before. I guess she means the extension behind the garage. Here's the guest room, or the only other bedroom in the house, as it's also known." He opened the door at the end of the narrow landing. "What the ... Mum! What is going on?"

Lydia pushed past him. "Ha, that is hilarious! Are these your posters? Really? The tennis player with the itchy bum?"

"They are not; they might just have been Glenn's. This is mega-embarrassing. Honestly, I don't know what she's playing at."

Mr Bellamy appeared behind them. "Your mother says could you hurry up. Ah, yes, the posters. She found them in the garage and wants rid. Being your mother, she decided the best way was to blu-tak them up and see who claims them."

Jake ripped down a Prodigy poster. "Well, they're not mine! Honestly, Dad, she knew Lydia was coming with me this weekend."

"Well, you know your mother. Feel free to take them down – you can answer to your brothers if you've destroyed their property." He wheezed a laugh and winked at Lydia.

Lydia nudged Jake in the ribs and kissed his cheek. "Leave them up. I'll congratulate your mum on her choice of artwork when I go downstairs. That should be fun!" Both men's eyes widened at this suggestion. "Joking!"

Dinner was laid out formally on a dining table in what Lydia would have called a through lounge until ten minutes ago, with matching Sanderson curtains, suite and table napkins. She wondered if this was the drawing room. The cutlery was laid for many courses, and Lydia guessed correctly that she was being tested on her table etiquette. She smiled sweetly at Mrs Bellamy, who stood at the head of the table awaiting their arrival.

"Gosh, how many courses have you prepared for us, Mrs Bellamy?"

Mrs Bellamy pursed her lips. "Please call me Rita. Now sit down, all of you." She motioned Lydia to her right-hand side.

Mrs Bellamy removed lids from vegetable dishes and a steaming beef casserole. Lydia picked up a soup spoon and then a fish knife and pressed her lips together to hide a smile. "If this is the starter, I'm not sure I'll be able to do justice to the soup course and the fish course."

"Oh dear, silly me, force of habit. I must have set the table for a full meal without thinking."

"Easily done," agreed Lydia.

Mr Bellamy tucked his napkin into his shirt collar.

"Colin! Please!" said Mrs Bellamy, and mimed yanking an imaginary piece of cloth from her chest.

"Where's Lucky?" asked Jake.

"Now, Jake, you know we don't allow the dog into the dining area when we are eating."

"Perhaps she's in the drawing room?" suggested Lydia, innocently.

"She is in the utility room." Mrs Bellamy informed her. "She's getting so old, she's probably asleep and not even aware you've arrived."

Jake had already stood up and was heading towards the kitchen. "Lucky, Lucky, old girl, come on!"

Mrs Bellamy sighed. "Jake, your dinner! This is no way to behave in front of guests."

"Mrs Bel – I mean, Rita, it's fine. I'm a dog lover as well. I've been looking forward to meeting Jake's dog."

"He could have waited."

Jake had returned with an old golden retriever wagging her tail behind him. "She was locked in! And whining! Mum, since when did she live in the lean-to?"

Mrs Bellamy glanced quickly at Lydia. "It's not a lean-to, it's the utility room, and that's where most people keep their pets."

"But it's not heated, or even carpeted. It's practically outside!"

Mrs Bellamy rapped the table. "Jake, can this not wait? Alright, let the dog stay while we have dinner. But could we now start behaving like civilised human beings?"

"Quite right, love. Now, come on, Lydia, help yourself to potatoes, and I'll dish the beef up."

Lydia became convinced during the course of the meal that Mrs Bellamy waited until Lydia had her mouth full before asking her about her job, her parents and her family home. When the meal was finally over, Mr Bellamy offered to make coffees and take them into 'the drawing room'. Something about the way he paused before the word told Lydia it was not the room's usual description. The drawing room was entered through a door to the side of the kitchen. The worktops and sink were piled high with pots and pans from dinner preparation.

"Can I help you wash up, Rita?" Lydia offered.

"No, thank you. Colin and Jake will do that while we get to know each other better, my dear."

Lydia hoped her feelings about this further interrogation did not show on her face. She was glad to escape to bed as soon after ten-thirty as politeness allowed; she had had job interviews that had been less gruelling. Mrs Bellamy's raised eyebrow at some of her responses had made it clear that Lydia's background was not quite as *'comme il faut'* as Mrs Bellamy might have wished. Several times she had compared Lydia's background to that of Jake's older brothers' partners as in: "Manchester University? Glenn's wife went to Cambridge, of course." "Eight GCSEs? I believe Charlotte got ten, but then she did go to a grammar school, you know." And Jake had been no help, too busy fussing over his old pet.

The next morning was bright and sunny. Jake had woken Lydia with a knock on her bedroom door, a cup of tea and a kiss. Lydia had pulled back the sheets for him to snuggle in, but he had backed off. "Are you mad? I thought you met my mother last night." Lydia blew a raspberry at him and slurped her tea loudly.

Downstairs, Mrs Bellamy was already busy in her garden and breakfast was laid out on the dining table and sideboard, as if in a country hotel. Mr Bellamy invited Lydia to join him on the boat later in the morning. Lydia shook her head. "I'm no sailor, Mr Bellamy." He leaned forward and whispered conspiratorially: "Rita wants a quiet hour or so with Jake. We'll say boat, but we can do pub lunch, if you'd prefer."

Lydia raised a conspiratorial eyebrow and nodded her agreement. She took out the breakfast things into the kitchen, prepared to wash up this morning. Mrs Bellamy was washing clothes in the sink and looked flustered at being caught.

"Oh, I'm sorry, Rita. I didn't mean to disturb you. Can I help?"

"No, dear. But could you get Jake for me?" Her hands held the items under the soapy water.

Lydia walked back through the lounge door and told Jake his mum wanted him, then followed him back.

"Jake, wring these out for me, dear." His mother held up some beige woollens.

"I could have done that for you, Rita."

"No need. Jake can do it."

Jake had snapped on rubber gloves and was squeezing the water out of the bulky items while Mrs Bellamy ran another bowl of water, presumably to rinse them as the next step. Lydia tried again. "Can I help at all?"

"No, dear. I'm just making the best use of my baby boy's strong muscles while I still have him."

"O-kay. I'll get my book for a read, I guess." No answer. She had left her handbag in the drawing room the night before, so she settled herself there and snapped on her headphones to drown out the silence.

It was half an hour later before Mr Bellamy popped his head around the door. "Hello, here you are. We've been looking for you. We don't normally use this room during the day. No need to look so startled, it's not a crime – yet. Jake said to tell you he has taken Lucky out and I'm ready for a –" he winked, "boat trip."

Disappointed that Jake had left the house without finding her, Lydia grabbed her jacket and followed Mr Bellamy out.

Once settled with a half lager in an old coaching inn, Mr Bellamy, away from the constraints of his wife, proved an entertaining and popular customer in the pub. "We should be back by three-thirty." He pushed his empty plate away and wiped froth from his mouth with his paper napkin. "Now, Rita is using this time to give Jake some upsetting information. Lucky is coming to her end, I'm afraid. Cancer, I think, so you may find the house a little fraught on our return."

"Oh my God, Col, cancer!" By her third lager, Mr Bellamy had become Col. "What sort of cancer?"

Colin scratched the back of his head. "Not too sure, love. Rita sorted it all out, vets and stuff, you know. Her department, not mine."

The house was sombre and shadowed as if even the furniture felt the effect of the shared bad news. Jake was in the lounge, Lucky's head on his lap. They both stood up as Lydia and Colin entered the room. Jake's eyes were red-rimmed. Lydia gave him a tight hug, and Colin patted him on the back. Mrs Bellamy came into the room, and they all moved apart. She looked more stiff and starched than before, a feat Lydia would have thought impossible.

"Finally back, then, you two? How was the boat?" They mumbled okays and avoided each other's eyes. Lydia suspected Mrs Bellamy was not fooled for a second. "Tea or coffee?"

"Can I help?" Lydia followed Mrs Bellamy out without waiting for an answer. Lucky followed behind, tail wagging hopefully. Once in the kitchen, Mrs Bellamy closed the door. "Colin told you, did he? Jake took it hard; he was always too soft on that dog."

Lydia was kneeling down, fondling the dog's silky ears and running her hands along the dog's sides. "Are you sure, Mrs – Rita? She seems in such good condition."

"Well, that's no clue, is it?"

Lydia was examining the dog's teeth and gums. "What sort of cancer is it?"

"A tumour, you know, an age thing."

"Poor thing! How could you tell?"

"The vet knows what he's doing!"

"Sure, sorry. I'm just shocked, is all. And poor Jake!"

"He should have moved on at his age. It's not as if he's here all the time. It's Colin and I who have to look after Lucky, take her for walks, feed her, groom her."

"Yea-eah. Did they take blood tests, was that how it showed up?"

"Are you suddenly an expert in dog cancer?"

"Ha! No, but my uncle's a vet, and we used to help out in his surgery at the weekends."

"You never mentioned it last night."

"I guess you never asked."

"Yes, they took blood tests. Her, erm, white blood cells were up, and she was off her food. Diarrhoea as well, of course. That's why she's in the utility room."

"On the concrete floor, yes. Did they notice the yellow in her eyes?" Lydia was checking the dog's eyes as she spoke. "And the furring on her tongue?"

"Yes," Mrs Bellamy sounded relieved. "Yes, all of them."

"Mm. Well, no doubts then. Shall I put the kettle on?"

Mrs Bellamy shooed her away, and Lydia made her way back to the lounge, Lucky plodding alongside. She pulled Jake from his chair and asked for a word outside. Once in the front garden, Lydia grasped both his hands. "Jake, I think Lucky's OK. Honestly! If you like, we can take her back to Bristol with us, get my uncle to give a second opinion."

He looked confused.

"I asked your mum about the symptoms, and she agreed with every one I mentioned. But get this, Lucky doesn't have them all and a couple I made up. I think she's just sick of having a dog!"

Jake pulled his hands away and stared at her in horror. "What are you saying, Lydia? Jesus, I know my mother can be a bit cold but, seriously, you're accusing her of murder, well, practically. Christ!" He pushed past her and back into the house.

Lydia stayed outside a moment longer then went upstairs. She went to her room, expecting and hoping that Jake would soon knock on the door to encourage her back down. Eventually, she fell asleep. She awoke to a late afternoon light, the smell of roasting chicken, and a decision made. She packed her few items into her holdall and heading downstairs, dropped it by the hall door.

All the doors were shut, but when she opened the lounge door, she found the table set for dinner and Colin dozing in an armchair. Through the back garden window, she could see Mrs Bellamy, busy with secateurs in hand, snapping away at the borders. Jake trailed behind her collecting the debris in a black bin bag. Lucky sniffed at the decapitated blooms at his feet.

Lydia touched Colin's shoulder, and he awoke with a startled grunt. "Sorry, Colin, I've had a text from my boss. I need to get back tonight for an early meeting tomorrow. Would you mind if Jake and I head off?"

He patted her hand. "That's a shame, love. You'll be missing a good roast dinner. Can you wait until afterwards?"

"No, sorry, I want to be home before dark. And I need to do some prep work for the meeting." Colin padded to the window and knocked on the glass. The two in the garden turned their heads.

"Rita will be so disappointed," he said, in a tone that suggested trouble was ahead. Lydia's expression behind him suggested she was ready for trouble.

"I'll go and tell her." She went out, through the kitchen, into the glass-paned utility room and out into the back garden. Jake's eyes met hers briefly as she repeated her lie. Mrs Bellamy was indignant. "What sort of a boss calls his staff on a Sunday afternoon like that?"

"My boss," Lydia answered firmly. "Jake can come with me or perhaps Col - Mr Bellamy can give him a lift to the station tomorrow morning?" She knew by Jake's closed-in face that he did not believe her, and she suddenly realised that she didn't really care, nor did she want him in her car for a long, sullen drive back home. She held out her hand to his mother. "Well, it looks like Jake is staying. Lovely to meet you, Mrs Bellamy. Jake?" She was tempted to offer him a brisk handshake as well.

"See your friend to the door, Jake." Was there a hint of glee in that remark?

Jake led the way; Lucky followed them. Jake picked up Lydia's bag and opened the front door. She clicked her key fob and opened the passenger door before taking her bag from him. Both stood for a second, actors waiting for the next cue. "Last chance, Jake," Lydia said softly. He shook his head, his eyes on the ground. "I'm sorry," she said.

"Me, too. You just don't understand ..."

"Oh, I think I do. Still ..." Again, silence. "Goodbye then, Jake."

He lifted a defeated hand and went back through the front door. Lucky was sniffing at an invisible trail on the gravelled drive. Lydia made kissing noises to the dog who ambled over. "In you go, Lucky, quick!" But she motioned to the open car door, not the half-open house door. Lucky jumped in, tail wagging harder, and Lydia jumped into the driver's side.

She rubbed behind the dog's ear. "Well, either way, I guess this is the end of a beautiful relationship, Lucky. Let's get you to Bristol and worry about both our futures after that, eh?"

And with a roar of the engine and a fusillade of gravel from the spinning tyres, she accelerated away.

The Clock's Ticking

BY CAROLINE TRAVIS

"No, really, Ben. I can't thank you enough." Penny's heart seemed to flutter slightly every time he'd come this close.

Ben reached for the handle and pulled the front door open. His close-cut white hair almost looked like fur, and again, she felt the urge to slide her fingers through it. As her cheeks started to burn, she reached for his hand instead and pushed a folded twenty-pound note into it.

"You've both been absolute treasures. Please, have a drink on me."

"Both of you," she added quickly, suddenly worrying that he might think it was all for him and then mentally slapping herself; maybe she should have given them twenty each.

"Perhaps not till you've taken the lorry back though." She laughed nervously, her face reigniting.

"That's very kind of you, erm, Miss."

Penny's tummy lurched.

"Penny," she reminded him for the umpteenth time.

"Our pleasure, Miss – erm – Penny."

'Oh well,' she thought. 'He's probably happily married with a dozen noisy kids.'

Ben shook his head slightly and took a breath as though about to reveal something stunning. He paused. Half of his breath slipped through his lips, and his frame seemed to shrink a little.

"Yes, erm. Right, yes. If you could see your way to popping a review online, me and the lad would be grateful." Missing the doorframe by a hair, he stooped his six-foot, wiry frame and stepped out of the cottage.

"Absolutely. As soon as I'm sorted." He was already down the path and out of the gate before she'd finished.

Penny waited for the vehicle to pull away, and as Ben touched his imaginary cap with his forefinger, she raised her hand and smiled, transforming her otherwise plain face.

Stepping back inside, she felt a small pang.

'Even if he wasn't ...' She gently pushed the door to and leaning against it, closed her eyes, '... he probably wouldn't be interested, anyway.'

"Now stop that." She said out loud. She took a long, slow breath, breathing in her new home, and felt her buzz returning.

Opening her eyes, another smile spread across her face as the golden-hour sunshine permeated the back of the cottage, filling her soul with light.

"This time," she crossed the fingers of both hands, "it's going to be all right."

She pushed herself off the door and moved, deliberately and decisively, to the box on the breakfast bar. She picked off the brown tape and liberated a large, bulbous wineglass from which she polished away imaginary grime. Putting the glass down, she stroked the wood-effect laminate and whispered: "Hello, breakfast bar."

From her shopping bag, she produced a bottle of red wine, twisted off the cap and poured a quarter of the contents into her glass. She lifted it to her nose and inhaled the fruity aroma. Holding it up to the window, she felt a warmth from the red glow.

"To you and me," she said to the house, and taking a large sip, she encouraged the earthy velvet to trickle past every taste-bud before letting it slowly slide down her throat.

Her phone beeped a coded reminder: *20:00 Invocation.*

She took another sip of wine and went in search of the box with the bits she was going to need. She thought about her forthcoming undertaking as she inspected labels on the stacked boxes whose contents awaited relocation: novels, A-J and K-Z; photobooks; classics; travel; auto/biographies; other.

"Flipping heck." Penny groaned and went to the boxes on the other side of the room: CDs; more CDs; LPs; FRAGILE; Ck Bs.

She stood, rubbed her back and sighed loudly. She checked the labels again, this time chanting 'New Age' as though saying the words would manifest the box. Finally accepting that it wasn't going to materialise, she carried the box of cookbooks to the kitchen and checked the boxes there.

Penny searched every label, finding pots, pans, crockery and cutlery. She could feel the old internal itch slowly pushing out the sunshine in her solar plexus and ran her hand through her hair before viciously scratching her head.

"Ouch! You stupid woman. I thought we weren't going to do that anymore." She winced slightly as she probed the damaged skin.

"Take a deep breath, count to ten and then check the boxes upstairs," she instructed as though she were calming someone else.

Penny stood stock-still, closed her eyes, and sucked in the air until she felt dizzy. Slowly, she released the breath through the 'O' left by her lips. As the need for more air forced her to breathe in again, the door-bell rang.

Torn between the need to find her box and the pleasure of her first visitor, she fabricated a bright smile before investigating the intrusion. She put her eye to the peephole and immediately recognised the back of the short, purple rinsed, perfectly coiffured hair.

"Penelope, dear."

Penny winced slightly as her immaculately dressed mother shuffled past her carrying a large casserole dish.

"I've been trying to call you, all day. Why in heaven's name are you not answering your phone?" She didn't wait for an answer. "I'm guessing you haven't eaten anything yet today? Where's the kitchen? Through here?" Violet bustled through and plonked the dish down next to Penny's glass of wine, her bracelets clanging like church bells.

She tutted and looked around the room as if it might fall in on her at any moment. "So - this is the little *jewel* you've been going on about." She shoved a box further down the worktop and placed her handbag in its space.

"Good gracious, child. What have you been doing?"

"You would not believe the day I've had, Mother. At one point I thought I might not get possession until after Easter." Penny dug her nails into her palms and swallowed her sigh.

"Well, you're in now, dear." Violet patted her daughter on the shoulder. "Though I can't imagine what the urgency was."

"Because now I've got the whole of the Easter weekend to get straight," Penny snapped.

"Well." Violet gently rubbed her daughter's back. "Welcome to your new home, sweetheart," She waited a moment before adding; "You look exhausted, dear." Her eyes scanned the rustic little kitchen a little more kindly. "And it looks like you've rather got your work cut out."

Penny silently counted to ten.

"Right. First, you're going to eat something and then I'll give you a hand to sort the kitchen and bedroom."

"Thanks, Mum." Penny squeezed her mother's arm. "I'll get plates and forks."

Violet popped the dish in the microwave and while the food was warming, opened the cupboard nearest to her.

"Looks like they gave the kitchen a good scrub." She looked into another. "You should still clean them again, though." She opened a third. "There's something in this one."

Violet pulled out two tiny, foil trays.

"Mmm. One used and one unused night-light." She lifted the unused one to her nose and inhaled. "Purple and perfumed, how sweet," and slid it back into the cupboard.

"Just like you, Mother." Violet appeared not to hear.

"And there are a couple of sheets of really nice writing paper." she continued, holding up the bundle. She fiddled with the little magnetic paper-clip.

"What an extraordinary clasp. Look, it's got a trumpet on each side."

"I have a vague recollection of someone saying that the previous occupant was a musician."

"I think it might be a bookmark or something," Violet continued, heedless of Penny's words. Frowning slightly, she popped them back into the cupboard as the bleeping oven won the battle for her attention.

The aroma made Penny's tummy rumble. 'For all your faults,' she thought, looking at the older woman, 'you can do magic with a few frozen ingredients and a packet of sauce.'

Violet took a couple of mouthfuls, chewing them slowly and deliberately. "You know your problem."

Penny looked at her mother briefly, shrugged, and took another mouthful.

"You just don't make enough of yourself." Violet put her fork down and studied her finely manicured hands. "I mean," the pearly beads quivered on her chest. "Well. Look at your hair."

Penny tucked a loose strand behind her ear.

"Why don't you get it cut in a more flattering style, dear? Or should I say 'my little mouse'? And there's really no excuse these days for dull nails."

Penny flinched and shoved her hands between her thighs.

"Please don't call me mouse." Penny gathered herself. "And to be fair, Mother, I have had a rather stressful day."

"Now don't go getting all defensive. I know it's hard to hear, dear." She took another couple of bites. "Believe me – my little mouse – if you look good, you'll feel more confident. And you'll attract more friends to you when you're confident. Maybe even a boyfriend." She tapped her watch with a long manicured nail. "After all, the clock's ticking."

"You didn't have me until you were forty-five. That gives me a good thirteen years."

"Ticking for both of us." Violet reached over and squeezed Penny's arm.

"And of course, you weren't my first..," Violet paused as her voice caught in her throat, "pregnancy."

Both women looked to the floor for an instant, each lost in the memory of David, a son and a brother lost in the defence of his country.

Penny broke the introspection.

"Some people are just not destined to shine. You know, the grand plan and all that."

"Nonsense, child. That's your father speaking." Violet moved closer to Penny, and sliding her arms around her daughter, hugged her close.

"Each and every one of us," she added, her chin resting on Penny's head, "is a brand new and unique experiment." She paused. "One set of chromosomes mixed with another set and the whole lot is dropped into a situation, with not even the power to control our own body. The grandest the plan gets is to eat and reproduce before being eaten." She hugged her daughter again and kissed the top of her head.

"I'm so glad I have you close again." She ruffled Penny's hair. "We'll sort you out in no time." Without looking she slapped Penny's shoulder playfully. "And you can wipe that grimace off your face, straight away."

"Tell you what," she said after a while, her mulberry-coloured lips parting into a perfectly symmetrical smile, "when I get back from this cruise I'm going to take you into town and help you choose a whole new wardrobe." Satisfied, she piled the plates on the draining board with the pot. "Right. Let's get this bed made."

"I honestly think you should call it a night," Violet advised from the open front door. She looked at her watch. "It's gone eleven, and you look all-in." She embraced her daughter. "Your box will turn up. And if it doesn't, is it really the end of the world?"

"But there's stuff in there; little treasures like the pen set David gave me when I graduated. And the snowy glass globe that Nan gave me." Penny sighed. *'Not to mention my invocation and candles'* she added in her head.

"No point upsetting yourself, dear. It'll either turn up or it won't. You could try calling the movers in the morning." Violet pecked her daughter on the cheek. "In the meantime, you'll just have to make do with what you have."

A light popped on behind Penny's eyes, unnoticed by Violet. "Oh, I do feel bad about swanning off and leaving you to it," she added, in an attempt to take her daughter's mind off her latest obsession.

"Don't be daft, Mother. You paid a lot of money for this cruise. You can't cancel just because I've moved house." Penny grinned. "I won't let you back in if you cancel."

Violet gave her daughter a final hug and turned away. Penny waited until her mother's car pulled away before closing the door. Leaning against the wood, a slow smile spread across her face. She'd moved heaven and hell to get into this cottage by today, the first full moon after the Vernal Equinox. A couple of days earlier would have been helpful, but now that she was alone she could get on with it.

"Thank you, Mother," she said to the empty house, "You're right. I'll just have to make do with what I do have."

She rushed to the kitchen cupboard where her mother had found the night-light and note paper.

She pulled a pen from her handbag, and laying the paper on the breakfast bar, she wrote 'WANTED' in the top centre of the page.

Wracking her brains to remember anything of the dozen or so drafts she'd worked so hard on, she wrote a line, then another, scribbling out and replacing a word here and there until she had what she wanted. Finally, she pulled the last sheet of paper from the clip and copied out the text in a stylish calligraphic hand.

Lunation was at 23:56 - in twenty-seven minutes time.

She read through her script and smiled. Taking it into her new living-room, she sat on the floor with her legs as near to the lotus position as she could get. She placed the sheet of paper in her lap and tried to empty her mind before recalling the instructions:

'Commence this spell on the night of a full moon or on the first Thursday that you take up residence. The most auspicious time is when the full moon falls on the Vernal Equinox.'

"That's three ticks," she thought. "Will that increase the potency? I can only hope."

'Light a coloured candle and recite your prepared invocation once in each room of your new home.

Complete the spell only by the light of the candle.'

Penny read and reread her petition until her phone alerted her that she had ten minutes until the moon reached its third primary phase. She placed the nightlight on a saucer and, taking it up to her new bedroom, lit the wick. Its perfume filled her nostrils.

Switching off the electric light, she began her recitation.

> "Hestia and Vesta, welcome to my home,
> Bring warmth to my hearth, a castle for my throne.
> To every corner, your light, please give.
> Protect all in this building where now I live.
>
> Venus and Aphrodite hear my prayer.
> Find me a soul, a life to share.
> Make him exactly what we both need to grow,
> Two lives as one, new seedlings to sow.
>
> Philotes, I implore you, bring me some friends.
> Friendships that jealousy and rivalry transcends.
> Friends who are fun and actually care.
> Friends without judgement. Friends who are fair.
>
> To The Goddess Morrigan, I beseech Thee,
> Bring me a job that fulfils my needs.
> Find me a post that I'll relish and love.
> I commit this petition to all you above."

By the time she reached the living room she had performed her chant four times, and the nightlight's perfume filled the cottage. Standing in front of the little fireplace, she completed her final recitation like a Shakespearian actor delivering a soliloquy.

As the sound of the final word dissipated, Penny kissed the sheet of paper and held it to her heart until her phone signalled 23:56. As its ring ended, Penny placed the bottom corner into the perfumed flame and, holding it as long as possible, she finally threw the flaming sheet into the fireplace, all the time her heart and mouth whispering, "Please."

Penny woke the next morning, and for the first time in her life, greeted the day, "Good morning, world."

She kicked off the duvet and, bathing in the warmth of the early morning sun invading the bedroom, she revelled in the song of the thrush.

Presently, unable to stave off her craving for coffee, Penny jumped out of bed and into her new "day? – No, stuff it – new life."

She was engrossed with emptying the boxes in the kitchen when the front door knocker tapped.

When she looked through the peephole, her heart missed a beat before racing to a gallop. Instantly, she recognised the close-cut, white hair and the wiry frame, but his off-duty clothes made him look a lot younger.

Penny checked herself in the mirror she'd put up earlier. "You're on, Mother," she said to her dowdy reflection.

She pulled the door open. "Ben!"

His lips seemed to form an 'em', and Penny's body sighed.

"My sincere apologies, mi–" He stopped before the whole word slipped out. "Penny," he corrected himself. He pointed downward.

"I don't know how we missed this." His hand swept over a brown cardboard box with 'NAGE' written across it, before disappearing back behind his back. "I do hope there was nothing in there that you needed last night."

Penny's face split into a warm and sunny smile.

Ben brought his other hand from behind his back and held up a cheerful bunch of daffodils. "Can you ever forgive me?"

Before Penny had time to say a word, he brought his other hand forward and held up a greasy bag. "I've got doughnuts." His smile made her knees feel weak. "If you've got time for a coffee."

JENNY DEAN

Jenny is a member of the Bognor Regis Write Club, and enjoys writing short stories. Since moving to Bognor Regis, her stories seem to include the sea somewhere within them, probably a reflection of how much she is enjoying her life here. She has had other stories published in Bogor Regis Write Club's earlier anthologies. You will find three of her stories within this book.

She has an interest in knowing more about playwriting, and has written and performed a monologue: 'For Better, For Worse' for Drip Action Theatre, and written a sketch: 'Dead Funny' for the comedy night at The Waverley in Bognor Regis in March 2019, in support of the Bognor Institute of Laughter.

Face to Face

BY JENNY DEAN

"So. What exactly, is the playwright saying? What was his '*raison d'être*' for creating the drama?" A pause then, "You, the actors, need to know. It is your job to impart his work into a living form. For your audience."

Jodie's heart leapt and stopped at the same time. Like an Olympic diver bouncing high before his fall into the water. 'What a responsibility,' she thought as she subtly cast her eyes around the circle, anxiously looking for a face that mirrored her own inadequacy. She saw no reflection; she wondered how on earth she had been cast. 'Certainly not via "Harvey Weinstein" tactics,' she thought.

"We've had a couple of readings of 'Face Powder' now so, Jodie, what's your take on it? You are, after all, the star of our play."

Was she really? She, a twenty-seven-year-old, 'treading the boards' for the first time? She didn't know if she could do it; was up to it, even. She sighed audibly.

"Well?" Justin, the director said, sprawling back into the swivelling chair, arms cradling his head. "We're waiting."

Jodie's mouth began moving like a car out of control. "Fiona has much to learn. About herself. Her relationships with men. To love and respect herself before anything else." She felt the eyes of the rest of the cast boring into hers, like accusations of disbelief in a courtroom. She didn't know if she could continue.

"And?" Justin seemed determined to test her theoretical skills after drama school. It felt more daunting than performing her final piece.

"Or getting married," she joked. "Well … she's been abused by her husband and is now seeking a new start. A new way of being."

117

The director looked pleased. "Well done, Jodie. You're right on track. A play about abuse. Mistreatment of women." He paused and looked straight into her eyes. "About you."

Jodie squirmed in her seat like a worm burying into the earth. She felt uncomfortable, vulnerable as she listened to the distant opinions of other members of the cast. She felt the eyes of the figure opposite fixed upon her. She looked across. A man, late thirties, thick-set in a rugged handsome way, was leaning forward in his seat. Still. Silent. Jodie's unease grew like an antelope being stalked by a lion. She turned away.

As the production team petered out from their first meeting, Jodie wondered how she had put herself into this ridiculous situation. Did she really want a part so much that she was prepared to play opposite him? Had she only got the part because of his theatrical connections, his influence? 'But why had he chosen to help me?' she asked herself, throwing her saddle bag over her shoulder. 'Not after ...'

Not ready to go home, she ambled out of the Green Room towards the wings of the huge stage. She peered through the heavy red curtains at the wide open space ready to suck her dreams dry: a new star of the age, an encore of BAFTA awards lined up on her mother's mantelpiece and Jeremy's adulation. Could she really do it?

Jodie's thoughts were off again like a new monk learning to meditate. 'And it's about to come true,' she thought as she walked onto the stage and moved down the rake. Training in Guildford a while ago now – not RADA but still pretty good – and 'first night' in six weeks.

But it hadn't been as simple as that. 'As if anything was,' she thought, as her mind rewound the film since her studies had ended. When her world had suddenly tilted further off its axis.

Jodie had blamed herself. It had to be her fault, after all. It always was, of course. She hadn't intended to stand in a close bodily embrace with Jeremy that morning; the Underground was always forcing its passengers into familiarity. They had both laughed; started chatting about her audition and then alighting together at Piccadilly. "It was serendipity," Jeremy had claimed. And, after a latte and a walk through Green Park, she had felt the same. She hadn't meant it to happen. She loved David, after all. Felt confused for weeks as to what to do.

Jodie told him. Had to. Heart beating hard in her mouth. She wasn't a deceitful woman. "I didn't set out to let this happen. Life just does its own thing sometimes."

He had been quiet at first, calm. "I can't take it in yet," he had told her. "I thought we were different. Special." Then he had laughed. In a sneering, mocking way that she hadn't chosen to notice before. "But I'll be all right, don't you worry about that." A long pause then, "I don't know about you, though."

Then she had left him. Gone to live with Jeremy. A different world. City jargon, mega dealing, mohair suits and polished shoes. No avenue to a theatrical break. But love was there instead. Forever.

Jodie hadn't wanted the relationship with David to turn rancid; she still loved him. In her own way. But, since Jeremy, it couldn't be the same. This love was different. Equal. She knew that now. David, ten years older than she, an actor nearing his best and she, a theatrical virgin. 'What did he see in me, anyway?' she thought again as she pictured their first meeting at the exhibition. He, a guest of the artist in residence and she, the curator. Over drinks, he had invited her to watch a performance at the Apollo. She felt flattered, and it had gone from there. "It's so refreshing to be with a woman outside of the theatre," he'd said. "They're all so affected. Up their own arses."

'As if he wasn't up his,' she thought. But it had worked. Somehow. As long as she behaved herself. Did what he wanted. Played the supporting role to his protagonist. Little woman to male ego. Otherwise the bruises, the black eyes had to be explained away with outlandish excuses. Jodie had felt frightened, lost in a world whizzing out of control. 'If only I could gauge how he'll be,' she had worried. 'He's so unpredictable.'

She thought of the evening that she had come home with the news. "I've been made redundant. What am I going to do?"

David had been warm, loving that time. "Why don't you try for RADA?" he had suggested. Just like that; out of the blue, over breakfast the next morning. He knew how much she loved the theatre. Watching him in numerous productions over the short years they had been together. Knew how she improvised Coronation Street's characters while busying herself with the meal's dirty plates and pans. "You've plenty of time now," he had said. "And I have the money."

Jodie smiled to herself. There it was again. His money, not hers.

The acting journey, with her husband's erratic support, had been challenging but Jodie had survived. Not so her marriage. Now with Jeremy, she found herself an actor with no theatrical home. No Equity card. No job.

Despite her feelings for Jeremy, Jodie had felt disillusioned, flat. As if she had chosen a foolish path; that the drama of her life so far was all the theatricals she would ever know. Her theatre was 'dark'. Then, suddenly, David had called. Pleasant. Genial. "I'm starting rehearsals. We're short of a woman. Leading role. How about it?"

And that was it. She had auditioned, mind locked in a rubric cube, and oblivious to any detail. And she got it. The lead in a premier performance of 'Face Powder'. "I can't believe it," she said. "Is every other actress on holiday?"

And that's when she and David became intimate again. "It's not real life," he had told her in rehearsal, but she could feel his dormant love expressing itself in the script. It was all so difficult but necessary to Jodie's theatrical hopes.

Six weeks later, the team was almost ready. First night approached and, with it, anticipation. Anxiety. Actors, despite their overt confidence, are some of the worst negative thinkers. They are never good enough. In their eyes. And so, too, felt Jodie.

The audience, full to the top of the stage curtain, was abrim with noise and expectancy. The first night of a new production. A new actress cast opposite the elite professional. Husband versus ex. Love versus fear.

Jodie, waiting in the wings and on stage from the first page, could almost feel Jeremy's joy as he sat in the first row. Her heart melted as she watched him read through the programme, imagining his delight at seeing her name in print. *'Jodie Tate' plays 'Fiona, wife of Simon Fisher'* and knowing what that actually meant. In realistic terms. She loved him even more for his understanding nature.

Then it is time. No time for reflection. 'Face Powder' has gone up. And she is 'on stage'. Living. Breathing her part. Immune to her life. Trapped in her role. And loving it. Absorbed, the wife of Simon Fisher, the only role she is. Alive. Being.

And there he is. Enter stage right. He moves towards Jodie, ready to embrace her in his arms. Simon, her husband, her lover. But ... wait.

Something has gone amiss. "Your visage, as fine as Eve's in Eden's garden, needs no charm, no face powder to exalt its balm ..."

Then, as suddenly as the words are created, the actor grasps a tube from his pocket and tosses a liquid into the space between them. But no space at all. Hollering, Screaming. Pain. Anguish. Each rent the air as if in a chorus of denial. "Best of bloody luck with that one," whispers David. "He's not a patch on me." A dramatic pause then, "Perhaps a patch of face powder for you, though. A nice reminder eh? Of your first and only performance."

And that was all Jodie could remember. Nothing of the trip in the speeding ambulance to A & E, the immediate operation to graft skin from skin; to make good physical wounds. Emotions left open. Abuse untouched.

Jeremy sat beside the bed, cradling her hand. "We'll get through this," he said. "Our love is more than skin deep."

And it had been. Two, three years of surgery to make good Jodie's face. Never the same, Never without face powder. But now, David's revenge satiated and justice served on him, Jodie feels free. Free from pretending. Free to live. Free to love. Fully.

IVES SALLOW

Ives describes himself as a private person: his family describe him as 'an analogue in a digital world' with nothing in the way of personal websites or social media accounts

He will admit to being the mature side of forty, with less hair where it ought to be and rather more where it perhaps shouldn't. He is at that age when he double-checks his reading glasses are in his pocket before leaving the house. In the distant past he had one or two articles published in magazines.

He is trying to make time for writing the next bestselling novel, despite the temptations of the nearby waves, tempting him to sail or swim instead.

Jez's Wish

BY IVES SALLOW

Saturday was a good day. Saturday was the day Jan came around. He really liked Jan – she was a good sort.

The compost heap by the fence was steaming in the cold air – for all the world it looked on fire – and wisps of moisture drifted into the sunlight piercing through the bare arms of the beech tree. He'd planted the tree in 1967; it was crazy how big the thing was now. He smiled as he recalled Frank at the hardware store selling him the digging spade – he'd put it through the till as a trowel.

"Boss doesn't even know what a trowel is." Frank had laughed at his concerned face.

Still in the shed was that spade.

His eyes followed the sun's rays to the winter aconites Mary had planted by the laurel hedge – he always thought there should be fairies there, dancing and giggling as they chased through the yellow flowers. He'd told Mary, and she'd kissed him. The way she'd looked at him … his eyes pricked at the memory.

A few winter gnats were hopping in the vapour cloud above the heap – up and down, up and down, like miniature yoyos. His hand went to his face and traced a line under his eye where there was still a faint crease in the skin, even after all these years. He grinned: Smiley Johnson, three times in a week, Smiley had hit the spot with his yoyo. One a bruise, second a cut, third took it right down to bone. Stupid bets really – you catch me on the head, you get my dinner money, you miss once, you tell your sister she's going out with me. As if. He coughed up a laugh.

Smiley – "Hi, sis, you know Jez, you're going out with him tonight."
Sister – "Fuck off."

He shook his head. Lord, he must have been desperate, he'd seen Smiley knock a fly clean out of the air with his yoyo. Wasted on the young, all that testerone.

He thought and thought but couldn't even recall the girl's name now. Could barely even see her face.

A puff from the compost suddenly ballooned into the gnats, and they shot all over the shop. Must be like a bloody volcano going off to them he reckoned.

What were they doing, all those insects? He pondered. Mating? He wondered if gnats fell in love – bit old-fashioned that now, falling in love. *Apps* – that's what everybody used now, least according to the paper. He blinked slowly and mashed his mouth into what Malc at the pub called his constipation face – what the bloody hell *was* an *app*? Seemed to be all the papers talked about now, bloody apps. Bloody apps and bloody celebrities. Bloody world was mad.

The insects settled back above the heap. They looked like they were stuck in elevators, up and down, up and down.

"Whoa!"

A sparrow lunged out of the hedge and the insects scattered like fireworks gone berserk. Did it get one? Give that bird an app, he smiled to himself.

He wondered whether sparrows fell in love?

Did the sparrow just eat Mr Gnat, and Mrs Gnat was in shock? He stared at them – there was one bouncing up and down at the edge of the group – Mrs Gnat, lovelorn? Fretting how she was going to live without her partner or was she just thinking, *'Stupid sod getting himself eaten like that, now how the bloody hell am I going to feed the kids?'*

The doorbell pinged and he gritted his teeth. He'd been ripped off with that doorbell – only worked on Saturdays. That was the only day the thing made a sound. Not Sunday, not Monday, not any other day of the week. Just Saturday. He asked Jamie to take it back to the shop he'd got it from, somewhere called a net shop or one-line shop or something like that. Jamie asked why and then said the shop said that wasn't possible.

"Seems unlikely, Granpa, only working one day a week."

The doorbell pinged again. See … it worked fine on a Saturday. He asked Malc if he knew if there was a local net shop – "Might be a one-line shop, Malc," – that he might be able to take the doorbell back to himself as Jamie said he'd lost the address. Malc hadn't heard of it either, so now the doorbell would just be chucked. He hated waste – if he were just a few years younger, he'd have taken it apart, found what was wrong and fixed it. Nobody fixed anything now.

"*Ow!*" He'd ground his teeth and chewed into his cheek.

Another ping.

Blimey, calm down!

He threw a last glance at the gnats and tripped over a broken tile near the fridge as he turned from the window.

"Every bloody time," he muttered. He warned the tile with a withering look.

"No.....no, I don't want any sodding new windows."

"That's good sir 'cos I'm not selling any."

He cringed at the deathly smile cracked into the moon face in front of him.

"I find most people are short of money. Are you short of money, sir?"

"Yes. I'll take a hundred."

"Huh?"

"Yes, I'm short of money, yes, I'll take a hundred quid."

The gnats were still there, up and down on their bungees. Didn't know how lucky they were, not having bloody energy salespeople to get rid of. But then salespeople didn't eat you, not like sparrows. Just tried to eat your money.

Another sparrow shot down and soared away with a gnat-sized snack. Was it a Mrs Gnat this time? Was Mr Gnat now reeling from the shock of Mrs Gnat suddenly being not there? Jez felt for him, he really did. When Mary had gone just like that, he had thought his world had caved in, never known a sadness like that desolation. Yes, desolation, that was the word.

He made like a predator and tried to lock onto a single gnat ... and lost it. He huffed, concentrated and strapped his gaze onto Mrs Gnat ... and lost her. Up she went and up went his eye, another gnat dropped down, and his eye deserted her for the descending insect.

"Damn and blast."

Five times he tried, four times he failed – he just couldn't stay locked on. The fifth time he started to look, decided he was a pea-brain for trying and gave up before she threw him again. He needed Smiley Johnson, that's what he needed.

Samantha! He remembered now. Smiley called her Slinky on account of the fact his sister was slim, and she was a bit taller than him.

Smiley would've been a good predator.

He could hear him: *"No weapon needed, mate, I've got me yoyo."*

Skilled job that, being a predator – hard work. P'rhaps sparrows *would* prefer to sell energy instead?

He hadn't turned the compost for weeks. He should do it monthly this time of year. Mind you it rained solid last month.

Malc said people were soggy these days.

Interesting theory: if it rained a lot did people get soggier? Did it soak in and dilute their soul? Make them wet?

Up and down, up and down, they were still at it. What happened to gnats in the rain? Direct hit from a raindrop's got to hurt if you're a gnat. Would it kill you? A bath full of water dropped on your head from thousands of feet – got to kill you, hasn't it?

The shaft of sunlight dimmed and shrank and was gone, just like that. And the gnats were gone.

The garden fork handle felt like it was stuck to his skin. He took his hand away and examined it just to check. No skin was missing – that was seriously cold metal though.

It was a struggle, but he managed to throw the tines into the compost heap and lever it up.

"Wowza!"

How do you count worms? He started … ten … twenty … thirty … that was hundreds. Thousands? More worms than he'd seen before. Going to be great compost.

Ping!

"Oh, you're bloody joking." He checked his watch to make sure he wasn't going mad and had mistimed it – no, it was way too early for Jan, he was OK.

What a dilemma, he thought. A malfunctioning doorbell and it's rung twice in one day. Is there anyone there or is it just playing silly buggers?

Then it struck him: if it only rings the once, that'll prove it. A person will ring again. He listened for a minute – nothing.

See, I told them it was faulty. Bloody doorbell.

Then he saw it.

"Caught you! I thought it was you."

He made to go down the path, but the magpie was gone the moment he twitched his leg. So was his seed marker he'd left in the ground with last year's leeks.

What do you do with them? He wondered.

Hard plastic surely wasn't any good for a nest – anyway, wrong time of the year.

He liked to think they were tokens – after all, if gnats could fall in love, why not magpies? P'raps lady magpies swooned for white plastic labels?

Peg – seemed cruel to call him that, he did only have the one leg, but it's what he called himself – Peg used metal ones on the allotment. He smiled. Peg made a load out of old cans, and every last one was gone in a week – but then he disappeared for a week every now and then too, did Peg. Malc said he was visiting the institution, said the tan Peg always came back with was only burn marks from the electrodes. So Peg had bought new weighty, heavy duty markers. Tied each one to a stone - said they cost so much he'd have a heart attack if one went missing. Jez took one, one night, then they spent the whole of the following evening in the pub discussing it: him explaining that stones weigh less in the air, that's how come the birds took them. Peg deciding, "Nah, I'm going to superglue the markers into the earth, that'll work."

Malc staring at them, really not sure whether they were serious or not.

The bird sat in the big yew and complained at him. It must have had a couple of dozen markers all told over time.

"You a randy bugger?" he asked. "Either she really, really, really likes white plastic or you're a naughty bugger with mistresses on the go. Which is it, eh?"

He pictured himself outside Smiley's house, standing there all moronic-like in his best jeans with a big white plastic seed label in his hand. "You dozy bugger." He shook his head.

Youth *is* wasted on the young, you're not wrong there, Mr George Bernard Shaw, he thought.

Mary had worshipped G.B.S.

Chatter, chatter, chatter.

The racket in the tree snagged his attention again.

He waved a finger indicating to the bird it should wait. He rammed the fork into the heap and stepped into the shed and grabbed what he wanted.

"Here, look at this." he stretched up his hand, holding a stake. "Can't read? It says mangetout." He tilted it so that his white lettering was facing the magpie. "You're done, mate, no more plastic. You gotta think of something else."

He thought back to painting all the lettering. It had taken ages on account of the paint soaking into the wood so much - he remembered thinking what it must be like to paint one of those big bridges, the ones where you start again at the other end as soon as you've finished.

He'd told Peg he could have the stakes.

He watched the bird fly off, bobbing in the air like it was riding a switchback roller coaster. He wondered whether, far back, gnats and magpies were related. They looked similar if you considered it – big squat wings for their size, bouncing them along like they were on elastic. Aerodynamic as a fridge.

Fridge!

He dropped the stake on the ground and grimaced as it bounced back and tried to spear him in the leg .

"Twit … twit," he complained. He synchronized to his steps, *twit … twit … twit.*

"Bloody hell!"

The water was creeping from under the machine. He hated waste. All that water gone begging. Now it was no good as deionised water for the iron.

"Damn!" he cursed again.

He tried not to think about it, but it was like mopping up cash and squeezing it into the drain. He thought about putting it through a coffee filter to clean it but decided that was stupid – spend five pence to save one.

He settled his concentration on the fridge. "You'd love that," he informed it, trying to sound condescending talking to a fridge.

Keeping his eyes fixed on the machine, he lifted up the broken tile and dabbed at the water puddled under it. "I *am* going to fix it, you know," he lied.

He stood up really slow, even so, he had to grab at the door jamb and squeeze his eyes tight shut to stop the dizziness knocking him over. *They were working.* Something flickered in the corner of his eye.

*   *   *

"He took *all this*?"

The GP stared at the sheet they'd printed for him.

"Where the devil did he get it all?"

Jan watched his lips move as he began counting. The thin, humourless mouth began to drain of colour, the way her dog's marrowbone treat bleached as she cooked it.

You're starting to wonder, aren't you? She thought, delighted.

"There's seven dangerous drugs on this list … a thousand milligrams of morphine … *twenty* thousand milligrams of co-"

"I think he wanted out," Jan offered.

The doctor's mouth was now so pale his teeth looked like he'd been sucking chocolate.

Had anyone ever kissed those lips? she wondered. She supposed his mother must have. When did she stop? When she realised he was *wrong*? And how long had that been?

He'd unsettled all the staff when he joined the practice, they called him Dr Creep. Old Dr Beamish must have known he was rotten – said he needed another doctor and nobody else had applied. So he let him get away with murder. She fired a glance across the table and bit her lip, tasting metal – she'd drawn blood.

"You might be on the hook, you know," she told him.

Unnecessary, but very enjoyable.

His darkened eyes dared her to utter another word.

Pure venom, she thought, fighting a smile.

"It's all stuff he got from you." She was enjoying this.

"Not in these amounts!" he snapped.

A bit less venom, a bit more worry.

"He had a great day, went in the garden. He hadn't been that far in months. I'm pleased for him."

"Bully for you."

A lot more worry.

She tried very hard but wasn't certain she kept her smile hidden this time. She could all but feel the terror bubbling up inside him now. He was practically acting like a chameleon – as hard as he tried otherwise, his emotions were washing through him, writing on his face, changing his skin.

Terror, hatred, terror, hatred.

"How –"

"– did we get it?" she cut in.

She offered him the smile openly now. "I helped him. I'll deny it, of course. Went all over the place."

She imagined the GP as a bowl of blancmange tipped onto a plate. As fast as he was disintegrating, she felt stronger. She drew herself up in the chair – it felt like someone was holding her upright, on a cord. She felt ten feet tall. This was even better than she'd hoped.

All for you Jez, she thought, *all for you.*

She leant down and picked up her handbag, placed it on the table. He frowned. *Is there such a thing as double frowning?* She wondered. If there was, he was doing it now.

She unclipped the hasp and drew out a small sheet. She knew he'd recognise it – and he blanched. She let her gaze linger on him a little too long before placing the paper alongside the bag – and then delved in again, and again, and again …

"I'm sure you're counting," she commented as she lay the final prescription sheet on the pile and refastened the handbag clip. "Every one is genuine, and every one has your signature."

She'd watched the colours closely. He'd been pale, a bit grey, a bit white, in fact, every shade of pale she could imagine, now an island of pink with red aspirations flushed his cheeks.

"You bitch."

"See, the thing is you *know* you deserve it. You're so flipping keen not to do anything, you fire blank, signed prescriptions around like confetti."

"You bitch," he growled again.

"My, swallowed a dictionary, have we?"

Their eyes jousted for several seconds, and she savoured every moment.

"We all know you killed her …"

He looked baffled for a second. Puzzled lines furrowed his forehead before realisation flared in his eyes.

"Yes …" she confirmed, "Mary … his wife."

Wow, bluey-grey in an instant. Absolute terror.

She was on her feet, squared off the pile of papers and carried them to the door. It announced being opened with its usual complaining screech.

She handed them to the tall, thin man who stepped into the doorway.

"All yours, Detective Summer," Jan told him.

She looked back at the doctor and his mouth made to form more words, but nothing came out. He looked nothing more than a gulping fish, eyes bulbous with horror. She pulled the door back, just a little more. *That sound.*

It struck her how apt it was, that cruel whine of metal grating on metal. Harsh and soulless, just like him.

She wondered whether his cell door would wail and needle like that. She hoped for Jez's sake that it did.

ALISON BATCOCK

Alison has always enjoyed creative writing. She writes poetry, short stories, flash fiction and has recently completed her first novel. Alison is a member of Chichester Stanza poetry group. She recently graduated with an MA in Creative Writing from the University of Chichester.

Mirror, Mirror

BY ALISON BATCOCK

It was nearly two o'clock in the morning by the time I got home. Sue's leaving party had flowed on to the King's Arms and then to a small club in a backstreet I had never been to before. I stayed with the group because I was pleased to have been asked. They didn't usually include me. I had always been a bit of a loner. My parents dead, no siblings. A distant cousin in Australia was about the only family I could lay claim to. These girls I worked with were all much younger than me. I had nothing in common with them, so we rarely spoke and certainly never met for a drink after work. I didn't mind. In fact, I was quite happy in my own company. I read, watched TV and old 1940s films. I had no trouble in filling my time.

Fed up with listening to the girls' inane chatter and feeling older than my years, I left the club alone. No one said goodbye to me. I couldn't find an all-night bus and refused a lift from a mini-cab driver who leaned out of his car and ogled me whilst offering a 'cut-price' lift home. So I walked. The front door slammed behind me, but it didn't matter. I wasn't disturbing anyone by coming home at that time of night. Number 14 where I live is the only property in the terrace still occupied. The rest are boarded up or vandalised, waiting for the demolition squad. The developer is going to build a supermarket and two dozen 'executive' homes on this small patch of London. I'm still here because I can't afford anywhere else. Goodness only knows where I'll go when the bulldozers move in.

The bedroom was cold. I threw off my clothes and pulled on my onesie as quickly as I could. I glanced in the mirror on the wall by the window. The bare bulb in the ceiling light made me look pasty.

I hoped the dark smudges under my eyes were only mascara, and that I wasn't sickening for something. I couldn't be bothered to go and take off my make-up. Instead, I snuggled gratefully under the duvet and fell instantly asleep.

The noise started at four o'clock in the morning. Tap, tap. Regular. Insistent. I ignored it and turned over in bed. I tried to sleep, but it was like Chinese water torture. Tap, tap. I stuffed my head further into the pillow and pulled the duvet up around my ears. Tap, tap. *Oh God, I* thought. *Not more squatters breaking in!* The last lot that got into Number 10 used to have all-night parties, every night – for six months!

After thirty minutes, I could stand it no more. I flung the duvet back and lurched out of bed. My feet hit the cold lino and I tiptoed over to the window, hauling back the moth-eaten curtains. The garden was shrouded in dull mist. The only light was a dim glow from the street-lamp at the corner. There were no street sounds. No branches touched the window. The world seemed wrapped in cotton wool. I shivered.

Tap, tap. It sounded as if it was coming from Number 15, next door. I padded back across the bedroom. Tap, tap.

"Go away!" I shouted, banging on the wall as I reached across to switch on the light.

Tap, tap.

The light snapped on, fizzled, clicked and went off again. *Damn. I've no change for the electric.* Then the bulb started to glow an eerie sort of blue light, and the room was slowly enveloped in a strange translucent haze. It advanced on me, closing around me, clutching at my clothes, breathing on my hair, pushing me.

Then I saw it. A face in the mirror, blinking at me! My breath caught in my throat as I stared at it. It was a young boy with blond hair flopping across his forehead. He was tapping furiously on the inside of the mirror.

"It's bad luck to see someone else's image in a mirror," my grand-mother had always said. Of course, she meant when someone else was standing behind you, looking over your shoulder, so that both images were side by side in the mirror. I don't know what she would have said about someone else's face inside the mirror, staring out at me. I couldn't understand it. I was frozen to the spot.

The boy waved and smiled. He indicated that I should tip the mirror up. I frowned. He tapped harder on the mirror glass and beckoned to me. I shook my head. "The mirror's fastened to the wall." I called out. *Now I'm talking to someone who doesn't exist.* "It won't move."

But the boy just pointed again and made a pulling motion. *This is stupid. Who is he? What is going on?* I shrugged and turned away. The tap, tap became a hammering. There was no way I was going to get any sleep.

I stood in front of the mirror and grasped the bottom edge, intending to play-act pulling it up. But as I grasped it, the boy kicked hard and the whole mirror swung outwards, as if hinged at the top (I knew it wasn't. I had fixed it to the wall myself with sturdy screws.) The sudden movement made me stumble. In an instant the boy leapt down beside me, grabbed my arm, and pushed me towards the mirror. My bare feet lost their grip on the lino, and I felt myself falling. I ended up on my knees in a square, black space, rather like a small cupboard. The mirror swung back into place behind me with a loud click.

I turned around, in a panic. The bluey haze was clearing and I could see my room – the bed, the curtains, my clothes strewn across the chair – and the boy, sitting on my bed, lacing up his boots. I pushed against the mirror's silvered back. It didn't move. My breath was pounding in my chest, and my throat was closing with fear. I kicked at the bottom, as the boy had done. Nothing. I thumped with my fists and shouted, but the sound echoed back at me. The boy pulled a flat cap out of his pocket, stuffed it onto his head and grinned. He walked over to the bedroom door and opened it. Giving a cheery wave, he walked out of the room.

"Don't go! Come back!" I screamed, slamming my palms on the glass. Sweat poured down my back. My head was swimming. I thought I was going to faint. An inky black began to run down the inside of the mirror, obscuring my view.

Then I was alone. There was no one around to hear me. There was no one around to miss me.

But I had to try. So I started. Tap, tap. Tap, tap.

ALAN READMAN

Alan comes from Grimsby but has lived most of his life in Bognor Regis and Felpham. A graduate of Sheffield University, where he studied Economic History, he worked as an archivist first at Lincolnshire Archives Office and later West Sussex Record Office, retiring from the latter as County Archivist in 2013. During his career he wrote and lectured on local, military and family history but recently his interest has turned to fiction writing, with the help of U3A creative writing courses. This is his first entry to a short story competition.

A Journey of Discovery

BY ALAN READMAN

I t was not the most promising of beginnings.

"The line's bad, Jilly, so let me get this straight. You're telling me that Mum missed her appointment with the specialist – the appointment we've waited three months for – because she was sitting at home watching a repeat of *Hetty Wainthropp* on Freeview? That's what you're saying to me?"

"Listen, Gavin, I'd arranged to leave work early and meet her at the hospital. I booked her a taxi, but when the driver knocked at the door, she sent him away. Said it was an *important* episode and she didn't want to miss it. All about an elderly woman who refuses to leave her run-down flat when it's scheduled for demolition."

"For crying out loud, Jilly, what's *important* about that?! She doesn't live in a 'run-down flat', does she? She's got a very desirable, detached bungalow in a secluded close on the Aldwick Bay Estate. Late paying an instalment of her Council Tax, was she?! The Council threatening to send in the bulldozers, are they?!"

"No. It's just Mum, isn't it? That's how she is now. If you were here and not on the other side of the Atlantic, you'd know that. So there's no point losing your cool with me, Gavin. I play the part of the dutiful daughter in *this* soap opera, remember? You're her blue-eyed boy living the movie-director life in LA."

He knew she was right. He felt the guilt. His mother was declining, it seemed, and it had suited him to leave all responsibility to his sister. She was the one keeping an eye on her while at the same time juggling a three-day commute to the office in the City and nannying her three grandchildren. He'd been away too long, hadn't been back at all in the last two years. He needed to take control. He made his decision.

"I'm coming home, Jilly. It's high time I saw her for myself. I'll be there in a couple of days. I'd be glad if you could pick me up at Heathrow."

She spotted him first. Dragging his suitcase through Arrivals at Terminal 3. Casual suit. Shades fashionably atop his balding head. The determined look of a man on a mission. She sighed.

After the briefest of greetings, she put him in the picture.

"Now don't bite my head off, Gavin, but Mum had a fall this afternoon at the bookies in North Bersted. They say she tripped. An ambulance took her to A&E. Her left shoulder was dislocated. She's OK, but they're keeping her in for observation and tests."

"Just a minute, Jilly, what on *earth* was our 85-year-old mother doing in a betting-shop?!"

"Putting money on Moby Dick in the 3.30 at Kempton, apparently."

"And since *when* has Mum been an authority on horse racing? How much did she lose?"

"Nothing. She bet £10 each way. It romped home at 50 to 1. She made about £350, it seems. Mr Maynard, the manager, says she's a red-hot punter."

They deposited his suitcase at the bungalow, then walked to the pub for scampi and chips, before Jilly dashed off to pick up the grandchildren from karate. He finished his sticky toffee pudding alone while catching up on the news in the local paper.

He skimmed the headlines. There was nothing that excited his interest: 'Birdman Rally set to Return', 'Felpham Labradoodle tipped for Crufts', 'Local Search for Unclaimed EuroMillions Lottery Winner', 'Bognor Rocks hit the Wembley trail'. When his taxi arrived to pick him up, he tossed the paper on the bar and left for the hospital to see his mother.

"Your sister thinks I am going doolally, Gavin. Set me up with an appointment at the dementia clinic, for goodness sake! *She's* the one who's on the brink. And do you wonder why? All that rushing around. Barely see her from one month's end to the next, these days. It's all too much for her.Dementia, *me*, can you believe it?! Just because I forget the odd thing once in a while. It's the privilege of the elderly. Doesn't mean I'm senile, does it? And now I'm captive in here. Had some twelve-year-old doctor fussing round yesterday asking me fool questions. 'Can I tell her who's the Queen's eldest son?' Well, really!"

"And did you tell her, Mum?"

"Of course I did. Charles Philip Arthur George, Prince of Wales."

"Wow! Was she impressed?"

"She was when I told her his birthday as well."

"You know Prince Charles's birthday?"

"November 14th. Easy, 11 and 14. They're two of my lottery numbers."

"Mum, you're saying you do the National Lottery?"

"Ooh, yes, every week. Same numbers each time. All birthdays. I've got Prince Charles; Shirley Bassey – she's 1 and 8, January 8th; and Alice Cooper – he's February the something. Tom gets the tickets for me from the Co-op."

"Tom?"

"Yes, that nice Mr Postlethwaite next door. Such a charming man. Lovely manners, so rare these days, I find. He takes me to Waitrose in Chichester once a week and does a few errands for me, now and again. Which reminds me, Gavin, could you pop round tonight and see if he picked up my copy of today's *Racing Post* from the newsagent? I need some proper reading matter while I'm in here. I asked the volunteer lady to get me something interesting this morning from the hospital shop. And just look what she came back with – pure chick-lit. I ask you, who writes this stuff? I could do better myself. In fact, I've been wondering about enrolling on that Creative Writing MA course at Chichester University."

He took a taxi back to the bungalow, just in time to receive a visit from the vicar.

"I thought I ought to pop round, Mr Symonds. Your mother was missed at Armchair Aerobics in the church hall this afternoon. Mrs Vaughan told my wife she'd had a fall and was in hospital. Would she be up to a visit from me tomorrow, do you think? It's the church's Spring Fair on Saturday week in the vicarage gardens and she usually supervises 'Splat the Rat'. I wondered in the circumstances whether she might prefer something a bit more sedentary this time, perhaps taking a turn on the Tombola stall."

He assured the vicar she would appreciate a visit. "I think she's getting rather bored in there if the truth be told. I'm glad to know she has such an active life at church."

"Oh, yes, Mr Symonds, she's an absolute tower of strength, especially with the Mothers' Union. The ladies are forever talking about the coach trip she organised a while back to the Alice Cooper concert at Wembley

Arena. A huge success. She and Mrs Vaughan had a selfie taken of themselves with Mr Cooper. It was in the parish magazine. Did you see it?"

Later that evening, after returning from the neighbour's, he telephoned his sister with his report.

"And, Jilly, there's another thing. Tom Postlethwaite, the chap next door, says he gets her a couple of bottles of sherry from the Co-op – litre bottles, mind you – *every week*! So, apart from the gambling, it seems she's also overdosing on Croft Original. I have to admit, Jilly, this has all been an eye-opener for me."

Putting the phone down, he noticed a U3A Attendance Register on the shelf under the coffee table. When he read the name of the group and saw that it was written up in his mother's hand, he phoned the number of the Bognor area secretary.

"Oh, yes, Mr Symonds, apart from her Conversational Serbo-Croat Class, your mother also runs two other groups – Bridge for Beginners and Mindfulness Meditation. They're all *very* popular. There's a waiting list of seventeen for her weekly Mindfulness class. I gather from Mrs Vaughan, who goes to all three groups, that your mother provides the most delicious pastries from Waitrose and is always *very* generous with the sherry."

He called his sister again to put her mind at rest about the Croft Original.

"When all's said and done, Jilly, I have to agree that whatever Mum's on and whatever she's getting up to, it's doing her the world of good. The doctor says she's amazing for an 85-year-old. Bit of forgetfulness but certainly OK to stay in her own home."

"Well, that's a relief, Gavin. I'd been thinking the bungalow might have to be sold for care home fees. That would scupper our inheritance."

After the call, he settled down in his mother's Parker Knoll recliner to watch the television. It had been a long day. And quite a journey of discovery about his mother. He caught the end of the regional news:

"And finally, the £73 million lottery jackpot is still unclaimed. It *is* known that the winner lives in the West Sussex area. The winning numbers again are: 1, 2, 8, 11 and 14. The Lucky Stars are 4 and 10".

A thought crossed his mind. He checked *Wikipedia* for the birth-date of Alice Cooper.

A few minutes later, hand trembling, he picked up the phone again.

"Jilly, are you sitting down? You are *not* going to believe this!"

Tales from the Best Book Club in Bognor

BY JENNY DEAN

1. MEETING THE CHARACTERS

Rhona cleared her throat.

"I'd like to make a start if everybody has caught up with the gossip. Sharon, that does include you, dear."

"Sorry. Sorry." A buxom girl in her twenties turned red. "I was just asking ..."

"Not now, dear." It was the leader again. "We have important work to do. Now, did we all read this month's choice?"

A man thumped the table and stroked his beard with the other hand.

"Right load of bloody nonsense it was. Gave up halfway through."

"I'm sorry, but I didn't finish it either; had to do an extra shift at Tesco's."

Rhona was having none of it.

"There's always time for things that matter, and this is one of them."

"Are you off your trolley?" Roger stormed. "*A Day by the* bleedin' *Seaside*. Sounds like a kid's picture book and it reads like one, too."

"Just because a title is simple, doesn't mean it cannot have an esoteric element to it," Rhona replied.

Sharon looked puzzled.

"Eso ... I'm sorry. I must be a bit thick."

Rhona jumped in readily.

"It's just that you haven't been educated to a very high standard, dear. Not your fault. You just have a lot to learn."

"Oh. Right. I'm sorry."

Roger had had enough.

"Do you have to keep saying that? 'I'm sorry.' Sounds like my wife's old record player."

Rhona attempted to focus the meeting.

"Please. Can we get on? What thoughts would you like to give, Sharon?"

"I did like the cover. You know. It was lovely and colourful. Those children playing on the sand."

Roger grabbed his chance.

"As I said. A child's book. And written by Harry Holiday. Do they make it up or what?"

Rhona, of course, had to justify last month's choice.

"Authors often have pseudonyms, remember. I feel it ties in with the title and theme extremely well. Linking of ideas shows imagination, you know."

"Sorry to interrupt but what was that word? Soodo? Is it something to do with Sudoko?" Sharon asked.

"Jesus Christ! Is it going to be like this all afternoon? I might as well go home." Roger really was in a bad mood.

Rhona, ignoring her male colleague, comforted Sharon.

"Never mind that now, dear. Look it up in the dictionary."

"I'm sorry but I don't know how ..."

Roger wanted to get on.

"It was too long for a start. How many pages do you need for a day spent on the beach?"

"The length is immaterial. A storyline can warrant a huge amount of space depending on the number of characters and sub-plots."

Sharon had another question. "I'm sorry but when you say sub-plot, is it like a substitute at a football match? My Daniel was a sub on Saturday."

Roger's face grew red.

"Lord! I thought we formed the group to discuss favourite books. We don't appear to have got beyond the picture on the front cover!"

"I see where you're coming from, Roger, but we're not all at the same stage."

Sharon looked upset.

"I'm sorry. It's me that's holding you back, isn't it? I haven't done anything like this before."

Roger was in a fit of apoplexy. "You're telling me! Why don't you just listen and let us get on?"

"We can do without the rudeness, thank you." Rhona felt in control now.

"Can we just bloody get on with it? Too many women and their emotions. I want to get down the allotment after this."

Rhona stood her ground.

"Gender issues are not part of our discussion today." Then, "So, what about the characters, Sharon?"

"I liked the man. He was really handsome and kind, rescuing all those creatures in the sea. The sort of man I'd like to meet."

Roger laughed.

"He's imaginary. He's in a book, for goodness' sake!"

"He was a hero, though. Like Superman."

Roger stood up.

"Give me strength! If no-one's got anything worthwhile to say, I'm off to my veg."

Rhona tried again.

"In my opinion, Julian, the protagonist ..."

"Sorry?"

"The protagonist. The one who leads the story. His actions were daring and exhibited his character so well."

Roger sat down.

"What? Rescuing a crab from a rock pool? Where have you been all your bloody life?"

"He did deal with environmental issues very well, and it was a lesson to us all."

"Sorry?"

Roger was on his feet again.

"Heavens above! What planet do you live on? Heard about plastic, the rubbish we put in the sea? Fact to fiction!"

Sharon felt perplexed.

"I thought the book was about a day by the sea."

Rhona felt it best to ignore the remark.

"Anything else, members?"

"I wondered what happened to the dog that jumped into the drain-pipe. Farfetched but ..."

"Perhaps if you'd read ..." Rhona was feeling agitated now.

"I cried," said Sharon. "It was awful."

"But was it pertinent to the storyline?" Rhona was enjoying herself.

"Pertinent? You mean, like when Darren says my breasts are like ..."

"I don't think we need to know what your ... he thinks, thank you, Sharon."

Roger grabbed his coat.

"I'm off. A rubbish book and a lousy afternoon."

Rhona attempted to bring the meeting to a close.

"A pity there wasn't more positivity about my choice but, with a second reading, I'm sure you'll see the complexity of the novel."

Sharon looked sheepish.

"I'm sorry if I messed things up. Does anyone want to join me for a walk on the beach?"

Roger replied scornfully.

"Are you having me on? I'm going to write my own version when I get home."

"Well, goodbye all." Rhona called after them. "Do keep your analytical minds active. Next month's book, *War and Peace*. Should be an interesting afternoon, don't you think?"

2. BOOKING A CHRISTMAS DATE

The lights were dimmed as they entered the Memorial Hall.

"Can't see a bloody thing in here," stated Roger as he peered around the empty room.

"It's all part of the effect, I suppose," Rhona suggested. "To create an illusion."

Sharon tittered.

"I don't mind. No-one will be able to see my spots. I'm on my period ..."

"Thank you," piped up Rhona. "I think it best to keep personal issues to ourselves."

"Oh, sorry. I was only ..."

"Well, don't." Roger was feeling impatient. "I thought we were here to enjoy ourselves. Book Club's Christmas outing."

"Of course," confirmed Rhona. "Sharon just needs looking after, that's all."

"You're telling me! Two shillings short of a ha'penny."

Sharon looked vaguely through her glasses.

"What's that?"

"Never mind, dear." Rhona was feeling conciliatory. "Look. The bar's over there. First round on me."

Sharon and Roger followed their leader through a meagre bunch of individuals sitting upright on plastic chairs, cuddling cocktails in place of lovers.

"What would you like?" Rhona coaxed. "Come on. It is Christmas after all."

"Just a coke for me," Sharon replied. "I get all silly on one glass of wine. Took my clothes off once …"

"God forbid! Spare us the details, would you?" Roger scoffed. "I've only just had my dinner."

"What's yours, Roger? Gin and tonic?"

"Pint of the best bitter'll do me. Thank you." And he nestled into a bar stool alongside a pretty blonde.

Once settled on a lumpy leather sofa in the corner, they took in the scene. Not really one of their usual venues for a social evening.

Who had suggested it, each of them wondered as their eyes peeled the place; an irregularly shaped wooden dance floor with an outdated stage at its far end. Frayed purple curtains swayed slowly with a fan's attempt at anticipating future sweaty bodies. Eight trestle tables, topped with cheap scented candles, clogged the empty space.

"This looks nice," Sharon mused. "I haven't been out for ages. Not since Darren …"

Rhona interrupted. "Thank you, dear. Let's keep Darren out of it, shall we? After last time."

"Don't know why we had to come here." It was Roger again. "I'd have much rather gone to the pub."

"But we haven't," Rhona insisted. "The Book Club needs some inspiration. Some food for our …"

Sharon was straight in.

"Did you say food? I could demolish some chips. With tomato sauce."

A booming voice suddenly interrupted.

"Could you all take your seats? We're just about to start."

The trio looked at one another quizzically.

"What's that?" said Roger. "I thought it was a Christmas dance."

Rhona attempted to acquiesce. "Let's do as they say," and giggled in her horse-like way. "It might be fun."

They made their way to the dance floor, each taking a seat at one of the trestle tables. It was all a great mystery. Next minute, the chair opposite each of them was filled by another equally imperfect human being.

The 'voice' yelled once more over the tannoy.

"Welcome to our Christmas Special – 'The Best Christmas Speed Dating Cracker' ever!"

The faces of the Book Club devotees would have embraced any front cover admirably.

"You what?" screeched Roger. "What the bleedin' …" whilst Sharon unwittingly adjusted her low neckline.

"Ooooh!. Perhaps that handsome man in our last book will woo me off my feet like …"

Roger had had enough.

"For Christ's sake! Shut up, woman, will yer," only to be hit with a stiff handbag from the female opposite. It was the blonde again.

"That's sexist," she ranted as he lay on the floor. "Your sort need to be …"

And that was the end of the evening as far as Roger was concerned. Out in the car park until the duo had finished. He took *War and Peace* out of his pocket and began to read by the light of a lamppost.

The evening inside the Memorial Hall began. Neither Rhona nor Sharon had participated in such an event before. It felt exciting.

Rhona, a middle-aged spinster, revelled in the attention – or lack of it, if she only knew – from young and old alike. She felt intoxicated by the blue eyes gleaming on her spectacles and the touch of a hairy hand. She began to wonder what she had missed.

"Perhaps we can exchange numbers later?" Humphrey suggested as the bell rang for the next session. Rhona was carried away like Cinderella at the ball.

"Yes, please. I've got it here," she offered.

Sharon, meanwhile, was equally transfixed.

"He's gorgeous," she thought as she kissed the acne-covered face of an overweight man covered in unidentifiable tattoos. "I'm in love," she sighed as she watched her lover wobble towards the next table. "My hero," she swooned.

Suddenly, the hall was lit in neon brightness and, the mask forsaken, stark reality reigned.

"Thank you, everyone. That's Speed Dating over for another night. Have you found your true love? Fill in the forms on the table to let us know."

As Abba's 'Dancing Queen' revved up into top gear, Sharon and Rhona sat starry-eyed. "Where's Roger?" Rhona suddenly remembered then giggled. "He's a dark horse."

The two women sat there. And sat. Abba turned into Tamla Motown then into Queen. No royal princes came to claim them. Two ugly sisters at the ball. Minute by minute, their full hearts deflated, let down by the two heroes they'd conjured from the page.

The clock struck twelve and the evening was over. Collecting their coats and clutching their disappointments like expensive handbags, they edged towards the exit. "Where the bloody hell have you been? I've been waiting here ages." It was Roger, *War and Peace* tucked under his arm then, "Did you meet anyone nice?"

Rhona smiled. "Heroes don't belong in the real world. Only in books. Don't you agree, Sharon?" And before her companion had time to comprehend the question, said, "When shall the Book Club meet next? Tolstoy is only Christmas reading, after all."

3. A RESOLUTE SUCCESS

The wind blew its deep breath into their eyes as the trio walked into its cold January face. Talking was nigh impossible as they wrapped their coats tightly around them and held onto hats as if they were the Queen's coronation crown.

"Whose bright idea was it to have our first Book Club meeting of the year out in the wilds of nature?" Roger asked, without expecting an answer.

Rhona gave him one with a smile. "I thought it would give us the ideal setting to discuss our last novel, Victor Hugo's *Toilers of the Sea*. Creative thinking, don't you think? And anyway, Copperfield needed a walk."

"Bloody stupid idea if you ask me. And what on earth made you give a dog that ridiculous name. Being imaginative again, I suppose."

Sharon joined in on another tack. "I ate so much over Christmas. I could do with a bit of exercise. Darren says I'm like a botox-filled teddy bear. My breasts have gone up to 38F."

"Thank you, Sharon." Rhona interrupted before Roger could lambast her. "Why don't we find a nice little shelter then we can discuss our book."

They strode along the empty beach, bodies bent against the morning gale. The sea, angry and grey, curled its upper lip in a mocking sneer as the waves pounded the pebbles like the lashes of an angry whip. The sky, dark and brooding like Rochester's brow, tossed its grey clouds across the heavens. Rhona, aware of her 'silly' idea, attempted to appease the group as they settled behind an outcrop of boulders.

"Have a good Christmas? Make any New Year resolutions?"

"Don't believe in making them," Roger scoffed. "Though Pauline's insisted I give one a go."

"What's that?"

Roger screwed his face up like a ball of pastry. "Wants me to stop complaining. 'Go with the flow.' She's got some hope."

Sharon perked up. "She wants you to take a boat down the river?"

"Good God woman! You get worse. Haven't got no chance with comments like that."

"But Sharon's just what you need. Gives you the opportunity to 'go with it'. Accept."

"When did you become a philosopher, Socrates?" Roger really was bad-tempered today. "Anyway, I don't intend to change."

Rhona looked at Copperfield playing 'chase' with the waves. "Careful, darling. The sea's too rough today."

"For heaven's sake, Rhona. He's a bloomin' dog, not your husband."

"She hasn't got one," Sharon piped up. "She's a ..."

"I'm not surprised, talking to a dog like that."

Rhona had almost had enough. "Can't you be nice just for once? Remember. 'Go with the flow?'" A pause then, "The book. The rescue was so realistic that I could imagine myself on the boat."

"I've never been to Guernsey," Sharon said. "Is it near Benidorm?"

"Why don't you take a holiday and find out?" stormed Roger.

Meanwhile, Copperfield was still having fun down by the shore. Although small, he knew no fear. He loved scratching through the sand and stones looking for discarded fish bones. He was so busy demolishing a delicious chicken wing thrown away by Mr and Mrs Thoughtless when the incoming tide suddenly caught him up in its salivating tongue and threw him up like a beach ball in summer. No-one saw or heard his distress as the dog was threaded in and out of the waves like a sewing needle through cloth.

"I think we'll leave it there if we can't agree on anything," declared Rhona. "I'm taking Copperfield home now."

But he wasn't there. She began to panic. "Copperfield! Here, boy! Here."

"What's up now?" moaned Roger as he and Sharon joined her. "Dramatising again?"

"Is Rhona in a play?" asked Sharon animatedly. "Can I be an extra?"

Roger's reply was lost as Rhona's cries of distress tumbled from her lips like a pair of pants in a washing machine. "He's drowning! What am I going to do?"

Roger looked at the swollen, icy water and sighed; he couldn't betray his gender, could he? "Very well," he yelled to the skies. "If I don't return, you'd better write a bloody book about this."

Hat, coat and shoes removed, Roger was soon submerged by the waves' white crests, being tossed everywhere like a marionette on strings. It was all he could do to stay upright as he forced his freezing body forward into the thrust of the tide, only to be pushed back, time and time again.

"Go with the flow, Roger! Go with the flow." It was Rhona screeching a song with the whirling gulls. "Swim diagonally. Copper's near the groyne."

Had Roger heard right? 'Go with the flow'? How dare she? But he could say nothing. He turned to face the defence wall and, body numb and shivering, he swam in tune with the heaving sea. Suddenly, he heard, above the cacophony around him, a shrill yapping. There, in the dismal light, sat Copperfield on the top of a breaker like a photographer's model.

Within minutes, the rescue was over and Copperfield was snuggled in Rhona's arms. Roger, exhausted, drenched and numb, stumbled out of the water whilst Sharon endeavoured to wrap her coat around him.

"What's the point of that, woman?' Just get me home, will you?"

The motley threesome made their unsteady exit over the pebbles towards the road. "You're my hero," Sharon swooned. "Just like Gilliatt."

As Roger muttered another expletive under his steaming breath, Rhona clapped her arms around his shoulder. "Thank you so much, Roger. Without you, Copperfield wouldn't be here." She paused then with a smile, "See. It does pay to 'go with the flow'. Doesn't it?"

JACQUELINE POINTER

Jacqueline has previously published two novels (one co-written with her husband, Jeff Ward) and a biography published in the Caribbean of her first husband, the Guyanese novelist Edgar Mittelholzer. She has also had poetry, articles and short stories published. She is at present preparing a new collection of her poetry.

The Woman with no Secret

BY JACQUELINE POINTER

On the train, I met the woman with no secret. Leaving my bike in Barnham station, I'd dashed up at the last minute, and jumped aboard as the guard blew his whistle.

"Does this go to Victoria?" I asked breathlessly. I was in trouble if it did not, for the train had started to move.

"Yes, it does, dear," the woman passenger nodded, "Though I'm only going as far as Brookvale myself."

So I sat down opposite her with my back to the engine, and we got into conversation. She explained that she had been to the market in Chichester for some early morning shopping, and was on her way home.

"I'm going to London to meet an old friend," I confided to the woman. "An old flame really." He'd been a boyfriend in my art school days. "I don't think it will do any harm to meet him." It had been my soul-searching about this which had made me nearly miss the train. "But it's a secret from my husband. I can tell *you* because you don't know us."

My husband was abroad on a business trip. At least, I hoped that was all he was doing. He never spent much time nowadays with our two children and me. Work as an executive, jet-setting around the planet on important business for his multinational company, seemed far more exciting to him than humdrum family life these days.

"I'm glad I don't have any secrets," said the woman rather self-righteously. "I have a happy family life. I have a good husband and two sons."

I could see that she had *one* secret. The roots of her immaculately permed blonde hair were dark. My own hair was dark and shoulder-length. Unlike the woman, I wore little make-up. We were an ill-assorted couple

– she in her smart costume, me in my jeans and casual clothes. I'd been told that I still looked young. Not that my companion looked old. She must have been in her early forties, same as me.

"I have a son and daughter," I replied. "It's nice to have one of each. But as long as you've got children, it's nice."

"A daughter! How lovely. I wish I had a little daughter."

Maybe my face was sympathetic. She glanced around to see if we were alone. I think we were, but our carriage, as was becoming usual, was built without closed-in compartments, so someone could be quite near you and yet not be seen.

"I did have a little daughter," said my companion, "but she died."

So this was the woman with no secret? The woman who had just told me she had a happy family life, as if nothing had ever happened to cloud it!

"I'm afraid it was our fault. We have a farm, you see. Rosie used to play around in the daisy field, pretending she was a little pony. She was very fanciful – I didn't understand it. We were going to give her a real pony when she was older. The boys ride the horses, but she was to have one of her very own. Girls especially like horses and ponies, don't they? Our Rosie did anyway." The woman fell silent.

"What happened to her?" I ventured.

"There's – there's a stagnant pool, you see. At least, there was. It's been filled in now. It's next to the field – at the edge of a copse." The woman could scarcely bring herself to go on, yet she wanted to tell me, but I had guessed already.

"We thought it was safe. But she must have climbed through the fence. As soon as she was missing, we thought of the pool."

They had thought it was safe – yet as soon as she was missing, they had thought of the pool!

"George, the labourer, waded in and found the little body, caught in the reeds." The woman broke down. "The pool wasn't very big or deep, but she was such a little girl."

A 'happy family life'! Obviously, the mother had never got over it. As if she could!

I would have offered her some tissues, but the lady was much more efficient than I was. So I was rummaging for crumpled tissues in my shoulder-bag when she took out her own neat box of them from her full shopping basket. She was not the sort of lady you could put your arm round to console – at least, not on such a brief acquaintance – and anyhow she had soon recovered her composure.

"Thing was," she resumed, "she'd never seemed like my daughter. I didn't understand her with her fanciful ways. She took more after Alan, my husband, and his side of the family. He was always the dreamer. This was why he started the farm in the first place, but he made it work. Only, he didn't take any notice of the stagnant pool.

"In lots of ways, I'm the practical one. I should have pointed out the danger. I always thought he favoured Rosie over Frank and Jimmy, the boys. But I was the one who had favourites. While they were at school or helping on the farm, she was too young. She used to play in the daisy field."

I suppose there were not always daisies, but this was how the woman thought of it. No doubt there were daisies when the accident happened.

"She used to play in the daisy field, which I could only see just part of from the kitchen window. And I neglected her."

"I'm sure you didn't!" I cried, partly because I wanted to assuage her sense of guilt, partly because, although she was not the sort of person I altogether 'took to', she didn't seem like a cruel woman.

"Oh, you know what I mean!" she exclaimed. "I fed her and clothed her. I left her to play on her own in that daisy field because I didn't understand her."

"You mean, you couldn't join in her games, how mothers sometimes do? I expect you were busy –"

"I didn't watch her carefully enough."

There seemed to be no denying this. A stagnant pool, deep enough to drown a small child, and the child virtually unguarded! But the woman showed *some* understanding – in the way she linked her *lack of* understanding with the un-watchfulness.

"She haunts me now," she said. "Often I look out over a field of daisies, and I can see her playing."

"I thought you said you weren't fanciful," I remarked.

"No, no, I'm not! I'm not talking about something I imagine. I'm talking about what I actually see – and hear. Sometimes she calls out to me from where the pool used to be – or from any pool."

A little shiver ran through me, not caused by the partly open window on that spring morning. Had the accident and the sense of guilt unhinged the woman's mind? It would not be surprising.

"Once," she said, confirming my fears, "I was riding in the woods, and I saw her little blonde head. Then I saw her face. I saw the whole upper part of her, high up among the branches. Her little hands were clasped together as if she were praying. Her eyes were closed, and there was a tear on her cheek."

I didn't know what to say after this.

"I'm glad I've talked to you," the woman told me gratefully. "I've never spoken to anyone about it before. Not to Alan or the boys – because *they've* gone all quiet about the accident, too. Now that I've spoken to you, I feel as if you've taken something away – lifted a burden from me. Maybe I won't see or hear Rosie any more."

Perhaps I would have thought of something to say then, but the train sidled into Brookvale, a little country station, and with a murmured farewell the woman alighted.

Ashamed perhaps of having told me so much, she did not wave to me, or even look back.

Somewhere a child was crying.

It may be hindsight now which makes me believe I had misgivings then. But I think I recall a sinking in my stomach as I sat there, waiting for the train to pull out of that almost deserted station. I thought of my own two children, being looked after by a babysitter while I gallivanted across the country, in search of a little illicit excitement. I resolved to get off at the next station and catch the train home. Anything could happen to your children if you weren't taking proper care of them …

As the train moved, I saw that the houses had soon given way to trees and fields. I looked out on to a daisy field, where I could see a little girl, playing …

PHIL CLINKER

Having recently retired, Phil is taking his writing a little more seriously. May 2019 saw the publication of his debut novel, *Bakerton*, set in a fictional town and revolving around the murders of a wealthy banker and three of his associates, published by Pegasus Publishers (www.pegasuspublishers.com), and available on Amazon and elsewhere. He is already writing the second novel in the series of three, entitled *Thurlow Junction*. Each book features his unconventional policeman, Sheriff John Withers, and his deputy, Dawg Janowski.

Beyond The Setting Sun

BY PHIL CLINKER

The view across the South Downs was magnificent at this time of the evening. The sun was setting almost in slow motion, its crimson glow seemingly burning the horizon, the great ball of fire itself half-submerged behind the beech trees in the far distance.

Marcia loved this view, and the time of day. She would often gaze from her bedroom window, absent-mindedly looking over the rolling hills and watching for a rabbit or a circling bird. She loved the silence and the beauty of it all.

Reluctantly, she pulled herself away from the window and moved to the mirror. With a frown, she studied herself, mentally picking out the flaws in her reflection. Her hair, she thought, was too long, and she hated the sight of those offending grey strands which seemed almost to reach out and smack her. In her mind, there were twice as many as there had been yesterday. She tugged at the ends of her hair and pulled them across her face, hiding the nose that she disliked so much because she knew it was rather on the large size for someone with such narrow features.

Her eyes were the wrong colour, and her cheekbones were too low; while, on top of everything else, she was too pale. There was no colour, no life – just a 42-year-old woman staring back at her, mocking.

As her mind began to clear, Marcia realised that she had been sucking the ends of her hair, and with anger, she pushed them from her face. She hadn't done that since she was a child, and, despite being alone, she felt absurdly embarrassed. To cover her confusion, she brushed her hands down her dress.

Her mood softened slightly because she knew that at least she had kept her shape over the years, and the soft green dress accentuated that fact. It was the dress that he had bought . . .

Marcia felt her heart rise, and she scurried away from the mirror. It had been about to reflect her soul, and that was something she just couldn't bear.

The sun was very low now; the red shadow had turned yellow, and one rogue cloud wafted across the sky, threatening to smother the disappearing ball of flame.

Marcia threw her arms around her body for reassurance, and leant lightly against the window frame. Her imagination was rampant.

He had caught her like that, not so long ago. What was it? A month? Perhaps slightly less. He had come into the bedroom on silent feet and had glided behind her, planting the tenderest of kisses on the nape of her neck. She had shivered and gasped in surprise, and then giggled happily. She had fallen back into his arms, and they had stayed that way for some time, each lost in the magic of the moment.

"What can you see?" he had eventually asked, his whisper soft yet hoarse.

"Nothing. Everything." She had looked back over her shoulder into his eyes. "Out there is the world, but in here I have everything."

They had kissed then, and he had spun her around and locked her to him. They had been as one, moulded together for eternity and beyond . . .

The doorbell chimed discordantly into her reverie, making Marcia jump. She stood motionless for several seconds until a further ring forced her into action. She walked past the mirror, stopping momentarily to adjust her dress and to check that all was in order. With mounting panic, she felt a tear welling up in her eyes, and she let out a deep breath before leaving the bedroom.

As she descended the stairs, Marcia could make out a shape beyond the frosted-glass front door. Robert.

He had stood on the other side of that door on Christmas Eve, singing carols to her through the letterbox. She had rushed down the stairs then, flinging open the door and laughing aloud at his appearance. He had been rather the worse for drink, with his jacket unbuttoned and his tie at a jaunty angle, despite the fine snow which fell over his head and settled around his feet.

"I'm drunk!" he had grinned.

Marcia had nodded. "I can see that."

"But I love you," he had added thoughtfully. "Can I come in?"

"Only if you promise to behave," she had replied with a smile.

"I promise." He had stepped over the threshold. "Well, I do live here, after all. A man is entitled to be drunk in his own do . . . doma . . . home."

Marcia had caught him as he stumbled, and had helped him up to bed. She had stayed with him, soothing his throbbing head and, finally, nestling in his arms as they fell asleep.

The next day they had woken refreshed and had exchanged presents, sitting on the floor beside the tiny Christmas tree. She had given him a volume of Rupert Brooke poems; he had given her his undying love – and the green dress . . .

The figure at the door was obviously becoming restless, for Marcia saw with some anguish that he was beginning to turn away.

She jumped the last three steps of the stairs and rushed to the door. Composing herself quickly, she opened the door with a gulp of trepidation.

There was a momentary silence as they studied each other. She saw again his deep blue eyes, his angular jaw covered with a less than perfectly groomed beard, and the mop of black hair, thinning at the top and giving him the appearance of a once-jocular monk, now dreadfully subdued.

"Hello, Marcia," he said at last, his voice faltering just slightly.

Marcia could not risk answering, so she stepped aside to let him in. Although he knew the way, he was an intruder now, and she felt she had to guide him into the lounge, where he sank into his favourite armchair without hesitating.

As he looked up at her, he tried a watery smile. "You're looking well."

"Thank you," she said primly, and a little more sharply than she had intended. She bit her lip and waited.

"I still like the dress."

"Really?" she said.

"It was always my favourite."

There was nothing more to say. Marcia retreated to the kitchen to gather her wits and make some coffee. When she returned, she placed the tray on the coffee table and blushed a little, realising that she had not even asked him if he wanted a drink.

"I've made coffee," she explained weakly.

He had moved and was standing by the bookcase, thumbing through one of the volumes. "So I see," he replied. "I would have preferred something stronger." He smiled again, and Marcia felt a shiver down her legs. It was that old feeling returning to haunt her.

"Robert," she started, but he wasn't listening.

He held up the book he had been browsing through. "Rupert Brooke – do you remember? He went through hell, too . . ."

They were silent once more, each knowing that communication between them had been non-existent even before he had left. Marcia sipped her coffee, her mind in turmoil as she searched for something to say. They had to talk.

Robert replaced the book and sat opposite her, holding the saucer but not touching the drink. She knew he was studying her, and she squirmed in her seat. He had never looked at her this way before; in the past, his eyes had been filled with love. Now, she could not detect any feeling at all; he was a total stranger.

Marcia stretched forward to replace her saucer on the tray, and felt his hand reach out.

"I'm sorry, Marcia," he said softly, and she knew at once that he meant it.

"So am I, Robert." She sat back, confused by his touch. This was harder than she had ever imagined.

Finally, to ease the moment, Robert took a sip of his coffee. He gulped it down, ignoring its heat. Marcia noticed the beads of sweat forming across his brow, and she knew it had nothing to do with the drink.

Robert put down the half-empty cup, the gentle tinkling of it against the saucer breaking the silence. "Marcia, we have to talk," he said.

"Yes," she responded, although her heart was not in it. She wanted him to take her in his arms and squeeze the pain out of her. She wanted him to tell her that everything was all right; that it had been a nightmare which was now coming to an end. She so wanted . . .

"I have some explanations." Robert was speaking in that soft, lilting way he had. At the same time, he was nervously picking at a tiny thread on the arm of his chair. His eyes were diverted from her. "I want you to know that I was never looking for . . ."

"Another woman? Isn't that what they all say? It was Fate that threw you together – two strangers cast away on a desert island of despair. You just fell into each other's arms."

Robert threw her a withering glance. "You're not making this any easier."

"Am I not? Then perhaps it's me who should be apologising."

Silence descended once more, throwing a veil over them. Marcia realised that she did not know this man at all, despite their fifteen years together.

Robert tried again. "It happened last Christmas. She was a business associate. Somebody invited her to our Christmas Eve lunch . . ."

His staccato sentences were like bullets, ploughing into her, causing her to totter on the brink of an abyss so steep that she could not imagine its full extent. But still, she had to listen.

"It was a typical Christmas get-together. Old Cooper got drunk, as usual." Robert smiled at the recollection. "We talked, Carole and I, for a long time. More importantly, she listened."

Marcia sat up. "Meaning that I didn't."

"Not when I needed you." Robert thought he was being gentle. "I was having doubts . . ."

"About us?"

"About everything. I had problems at work – but you never showed much interest. We seemed to be growing apart." He gave an involuntary chuckle. "I suppose they all say that, too." He paused. "I had drunk rather too much of some particularly rotten red wine; and, without thinking it through, I offered to escort Carole home. It seemed the most natural thing in the world to do. She invited me in for a drink . . ."

Marcia's face flushed. "And you came home to me, so that I could put you to bed and comfort you."

"I realise how it sounds, Marcia, but . . ." Robert's voice trailed away, lost somewhere in his throat, the words becoming jumbled and beyond utterance. Instead, he sighed heavily.

"Go on," urged Marcia, torn between wanting and *not* wanting to know.

Robert made an effort to control himself and looked at her. "She was different, Marcia. She was alive, vibrant. She was what I wanted, what I needed. She filled a void in my life. When I left . . ."

"Walked out!" Marcia corrected him bitterly.

He shrugged with resignation. "When I walked out, I stayed with Carole; but it was no good. The magic of the moment had evaporated. It was infatuation – I realise that now."

Marcia's heart skipped a beat. "You've left her. Is that why you telephoned me?"

"Partly." He hesitated. "Marcia, I want you to understand what I am about to say." He studied her once more, searching for a sign that she was aware of his inner agony. He saw in her eyes nothing to ease his burden. "I left Carole because there was no love. I left you because I *believed* there was no love. I was wrong."

Marcia couldn't trust herself to say anything. Her mind was in confusion, her thoughts racing off at all angles.

Robert continued, "I *do* love you, Marcia. Truly. But I'm not coming home."

She felt her body go weak and gave out a little cry. "What do you mean, Robert? How can you love me and yet not want to be with me? I don't understand."

"I don't understand it myself. But I know that to come back would be a mistake – for both of us. What we had is no longer there. It's over."

Robert rose and stood beside her. With tenderness, he placed his hand on her shoulder and gave her the gentlest of squeezes. "I'm so sorry, Marcia," he whispered; and then he was gone.

Marcia stood slowly. She shuffled to the front door and watched as his car disappeared from view, her heart seemingly in the passenger seat beside him. She closed the door and climbed the stairs. Stepping into the bedroom, she avoided the mirror and went straight to her favourite place.

The sun had all but gone now. The shadows were longer, but less pronounced. There was no sign of hopping rabbits. The Downs looked bleak, their warmth and colour shrouded by a night sky.

Marcia threw her arms around herself and leant on the window frame, looking out into the world.

And then she cried.

Only Make Believe?

BY JENNY DEAN

She stood quietly, her lean body pressed against the cold metal railing. Watching but not watching, trapped in her own tragic scenario. The wind whipped her stockinged legs as if scolding her for being there. As if she shouldn't be looking. But she couldn't draw herself away from the same picture she had viewed only a year before. The same black clouds, their fierce faces storming across the grey sky and the tumultuous waves lashing and beating the soft sand with their violent tongues.

The cold January morning had brought with it a small film crew who moved urgently and purposefully across the stony beach alongside the pier. A yellow tape, strung from one rusty post to another, screamed in the wind as it flapped like the wings of a hungry seagull wheeling above. A policewoman standing on duty like a bouncer at a night club. A small fishing boat upturned further along the shore. 'No Refuge', she read through watery eyes.

"It's uncanny," she murmured under her breath. "How did they …?"

Suddenly, a young man, dressed in red shorts and windcheater, his hair screwed back in a knot, shouted in competition with the elements. "Extras! Over here. Your job – gawp and stare, lots of comments and jokes as he's brought up the beach. It's all yours. Go for it!"

A disparate array of individuals, marched towards the director, self-importance written across their red-raw faces as they took up their positions. Lydia gulped. "There's even a dog," she thought. "How could they?"

Lydia squashed her emotions as she watched two figures, beaming in hi-viz jackets, scramble over the pebbles into view. Between them swayed a thin canvas stretcher. She knew what lay upon it without looking. But she did. Had to. The dark auburn head of a middle-aged man, maybe fifty or so, lolled from side to side like a rolling carrot, his face pale and still. She knew who it was. And it was too much. It was all her fault.

And the dog. She clutched the railing tight, her knuckles about to burst. "No! No! Please. No!" whilst her closed eyes leached tears down her face. "No! No!"

"It's all right, dear. No need to worry. It's only a film. Make-believe."

Lydia turned around. A man, whose face seemed vaguely familiar, placed his hand on her arm. "No need to be disturbed." A pause then, "I'm sure everything will be all right. They like to give us happy endings, don't they?"

She tried to smile, but her skin felt as tight as the corpse's fifty yards away. "I don't think ..."

"How about a nice cup of tea? I only came down to see that famous actor. You know, the one who's in ..."

Of course. It was all coming back. That was why she was here. Toby Jones. And the comedy about her seaside town. 'Funny sense of humour,' she thought as she turned her back on the scene.

The pair walked towards the café next to the pier. "A bit too black for me," she tried, "as you can see."

She wiped her eyes and sat down at the table nestling near a large window. Why did she need to torment herself so? What good would it do?

"Here we are, dear. Lovely cup of tea and two slices of my favourite cake. That should cheer you up."

Lydia looked at the man. A tall chap, about her age, wrapped in a thick grey overcoat, paisley scarf and trilby hat. "I'm Tony."

She knew it was before he had spoken. But how? Maybe she didn't; perhaps it was her muddled emotions making up another story, she decided.

"Are you feeling better now?" he asked when her plate was empty. "You were very upset." He laughed. "Those actors must have been doing a decent job to convince you ..."

"No! It wasn't that!" She spat the words out like a snake's forked tongue before she realised. "No-one knows the whole story. Only me."

And Lydia was back in her flow of tears. "If only ..."

"If only what?" Tony touched her hand again, and his eyes curled into deep creases. That was all she needed: a smile, a kind word, and a sympathetic gesture.

"Richard always wanted to be a doctor. At least, a vet to begin with. Right from the age of eight, he told me. Used to like healing all the animals. Putting a splint on a hedgehog's broken leg, tending a pigeon's wing." She laughed. "He even turned a lamb inside its mother's womb once. On holiday at a farm.

"But it was when his mother had a bad road accident that his interest turned towards people. She had broken both legs. Had internal injuries, too. Was in hospital for weeks. Went home, though, pretty intact."

She paused. "Richard was overawed by her recovery, he said, and that was it. Studied for seven years. Qualified at twenty-five. Some doing. He wanted to heal. Make people better on all levels – physically, mentally. Even spiritually. Believed anything was possible."

"And did he? Make people better, I mean?"

"At first. Yes. At least he thought so. Worked at a big teaching hospital in London. Keen to pass his knowledge on. His philosophy. That each of us is a whole being and we can't be healed completely if we're separated into 'parts'. But, after a time, he grew disillusioned. Other doctors scorned his ideas. Said they hadn't the time nor money to see patients in his way. Surgery had to be done in isolation. Illnesses needed curing. Patients wanted quick results.

"So he left after ten years. Became a GP. That's when he found it most difficult. Long hours. Too many patients wanting help. But not the sort he wanted to give. Time. Attention. Love. Instead, being a doctor meant handing out repeat prescriptions, antibiotics by the handful. Worse of all, for him, though, was most of the patients didn't want to help themselves; they expected to have unhealthy lifestyles and thrive. Not one seemed to take responsibility for their own health. He felt he was conniving in their own early deaths not curing them.

"It all got too much for him. That was some years ago now. He started drinking. Well, we all do that sometimes, but his was different. Far too much. And it wasn't just at home. Hid whisky in his drawer at the surgery. Dread to think what some of his patients thought."

Tony smiled, coaxing her on.

"I didn't realise all this at the time. Not to that extent. I knew he'd been feeling down for a long time but he never talked about it. Not really. Wasn't until one of his colleagues turned up at the door one evening that more came out. He was having an affair. With her. 'I wanted to let you know,' she said. Goodness knows why. Perhaps she thought I'd throw him out. As if I would. But I hadn't suspected a thing." Lydia winced. "Too wrapped up in my own little world. I could …"

"No point." It was Tony again.

"Things grew even worse. He was taking medical drugs, too. Stealing them. His way of blotting everything out. Coping." Lydia let out a wry laugh. "Ironic, don't you think? Richard, a doctor who couldn't even heal himself. Told me once, 'I'm only human, Lydia.' And he's right. Doctors are no different from their patients." Another chortle then, "We all suffer. Doctors have such huge responsibilities."

Tony was silent; who was he to make a judgement?

Lydia continued. "He was bound to get caught. I mean … anyway, that's when he lost his job. Sacked on the spot and down for a court hearing."

She sank her head into her chest and cried. "If only I'd tried talking to him …"

"What good is this now?" Tony comforted her. "He seemed …"

"He had such high ideals," she interrupted. "That was the thing." She paused. "He lost his soul and its purpose." Silence sat between them for a moment. "That's when it happened. I'd left him on his own one evening. Went out with a friend to the cinema. Richard never wanted to go. When I got back, he wasn't there. I knew something had happened. Instinctively, I ran to the beach."

She paused and looked out of the window. "It was here. A minute's walk from home. He loved the sea. Said it gave him his soul back. Sailing the boat, watching the tides turn and listening to the ocean."

Lydia sighed. "I could have helped him," she cried. "But I didn't. He had to keep working. Just to satisfy a life I had become accustomed to." She thrust her hands over her face. "If only I'd tried. Discussed things. It wouldn't have mattered, not having the money. But I didn't do anything."

A waitress, bending over to retrieve the used dishes, cut the conversation in two. Then she was gone, leaving a space in the script. "'I just want to be,' he said. 'Not strive for anything anymore. I can still be that healer, you know. In little things. A smile, a kind word, a random gesture.'"

"And?" Tony was listening intently.

"I laughed at him. Said he was talking like a child. Asked how he intended to support me."

"What happened? At the beach."

"I knew he was down there. On the beach somewhere. But I didn't think he would go out in the boat. Not on an evening like that. It was just like …" Lydia didn't trust herself to say it. "The sea was a bulging giant. He didn't stand a chance. Then I saw the boat. His boat. I knew he wasn't coming back."

"And the dog?"

She had forgotten. "He took Jasper with him. On 'Refuge'. They were inseparable. He survived. Jumped from the boat somehow and alerted a passer-by." A dark shadow smeared across her forehead. "But he didn't last. Died two months later. Missed Richard, I suppose. Like me."

Lydia looked out of the window. The sky was turning into a blue palette and the sea into a rhythmic calm. The filming had finished; the yellow tape discarded into a brimming bin, the policewoman searching elsewhere for a crime to attend to and the boat still overturned like a whale's failed somersault. The extras sat in the back of a white van on the edge of the promenade, drinking steaming cups of tea whilst 'red shorts' director, board in hand, completed the assignment on paper. It was all over. 'For them, at least,' she thought. 'Just another day filming. Another comedy. Not real life. Only make-believe.'

She came back to the moment. And Tony. "I'm sorry. Not a very happy tale to tell."

He smiled and took her hand. "I've heard it all before, Lydia."

She suddenly felt cross. "Then why let me explain it all?"

"Just as you said. Talking heals." There was a long pause. "You see, I was part of that story. I was the passer-by."

And Lydia suddenly knew his face. The one, along with all the others in court that she had blocked out. Until now. But she knew, at that moment, that his smile, his kind word and his sympathetic gesture were all that she needed to move on.

RACHEL ELLEN PENHALIGON

Rachel's family home is in Lezant, Cornwall. She is currently studying English at Chichester University and hopes to further her writing career after graduating.

Benchmen

BY RACHEL ELLEN PENHALIGON

I'm sitting on a bench in my local park. Not any specific bench, just the nearest one to the entrance that isn't already occupied. It is old and worn with very little comfort provided. I have nothing to do – never do. I place my overused back-pack next to me. The bench is decently shaded, and with the blanket I have stuffed in the bottom of my bag, I should be alright this evening. As alright as I can get anyway.

The park is a large open field with a little climbing frame in the bottom right corner. The nearest thing to nature this city has, though the grass needs some TLC, and they might want to consider hiring a litter picker a couple of days a week. The place is filthy, which is why I'm pretty sure I'm the only person here not buying one drug or another. It's amazing how quickly it changes: the every-day to the dangerous.

Mums jogging with babies in buggies, toddlers climbing random things and parents watching, hoping they don't fall. As soon as the sun starts to recede, families of all shapes and sizes get back in their cars, eager to get home before bed-time rituals are ruined.

Those are just the later ones; most pack up around three; a half-hour of silence mixed with wind whistling, and then out comes the hooded, pale figures. One by one, they all go up to each other, swapping rolled cash for plastic sandwich bags, full of God knows what. I'm not surprised the others left, I would if I had anywhere else to go.

Due to the season the trees are getting barer by the day, and soon winter will hit. That's the one that'll kill you: winter. The cold seeps through you, the bitterness worming itself so deep inside it gives your soul a formal handshake, and the unsympathetic wind, hitting you from all sides, as if it's trying to ask your bones to 'square up'.

I think autumn's harsh too, don't get me wrong. It's the slow build-up to the only show anyone's ever wished was anti-climactic; sadly it isn't.

I look at the leaves, half-crumpled, brown, almost dying. Reminds me of myself to be honest. Its veins are clear to see, like the leathered skin of an old man sitting in his armchair. Not quite crackable, still with a rubbery consistency, tearable yet not torn. The leaves tap along the floor when the wind blows, though fall silent when they hit the grass. I take a deep breath; their smell is like a good past time. They seem at peace though, as if life has been kind. Better than most I would think.

As people slowly walk by, some staring directly at me, some so obviously looking away, the crunch of the leaf-littered floor becomes quite loud. As the wind picks up, I get my blanket out of my bag and place it over my legs. It calms fairly quickly though, as the sky starts to darken, and the stars slowly appear. Every now and then a loud rustling sound gets louder, and I pause, guessing it's either a small creature trying to avoid me, or someone's loose dog.

I should really try and find a new jacket. This one has holes in it, courtesy of last winter. That was a bitter one.

Summers can be just as bad, having to carry everything around as if I need them. It'd be a stupid plan to leave things behind seeing as in the next six months I'd need them again. I've considered hiding them before, my coat and blanket I mean, checking on them now and then to make sure they are still there. The risks of someone taking or binning them are too high. I've also considered nicking someone else's jacket, though I could never bring myself to do it.

I like to think we're almost family, the other alone and I. I can have a conversation with any one of them, just to chit chat or complain; either way, they're happy to sit and listen. They even join in sometimes; it's usually the old blokes who do.

The younger ones just tend to wallow in self-pity, regretting leaving whatever they've left. Occasionally you'll get someone walking around with a photo looking for a nephew or a niece, the child of their disappointing sibling more entertained by a bottle than by their kids' future.

The saddest ones are the grandparents looking for their grand-daughters. You know she's not here; never was. She didn't give up on the family and bail or run from her failed education. I think they know it too, they just don't want to believe it.

"Have you seen this girl?" they might ask, putting the picture directly in a guy's face.

After mumbling a couple of times against his knees, where he sits huddled on the pavement, the man's eyes focus, and he shakes his head. The older gentleman moves onto the next person, going to and from every hunched-over figure he can find.

Eventually, he comes to me, asking if I'd seen her. Like always I would say no but give him a smile as he thanks me and walks away. After a couple of hours, he might give up, sighing, and call it a night in the hopes that tomorrow will take him one step closer to the teenager he's looking for; or maybe he'll keep looking, regretting how early he retired the day before.

The best types of people are the ones that somehow have musical instruments. They definitely add a spot of entertainment. I wish I could play an instrument. When I was younger, my mum paid someone to teach me to play the piano. It was OK for a couple of months, but like most things your parents force upon you, it became rather dull. Though if you sat me in front of a keyboard today, I reckon I could still jam out to 'Three Blind Mice'. Some of the songs played by others in the street are quite good, especially if you manage to sit next to someone who's clearly been playing since they were two. I'm pretty sure most teenagers who do it are just doing it for paid practice time. I can't blame them really, if I could, I would too.

The wind picks up again. Everybody's left by this point, gone inside to stay warm. I bundle myself up and lie down on the bench with my hood up. Listening to the wind I slowly start to drift off in the hope I'll wake up tomorrow.

LEN GOULD

Len has been involved in writing since he came to live in Chichester from London twenty years ago. For some years, he was a member of the local Workers Educational Association (WEA) Creative Writing Group. His output includes three collections of short stories, occasional pieces on sport and football and various sets of travel writing. He is interested in the space that frequently lies between what we regard as historical fact and how it can be interpreted in art. Generally, his themes concern loss, memory and the importance of music in the life of an individual.

Leave The Key
Somewhere Safe

BY LEN GOULD

L a Macarena was a café on Moscow Road, in the Queensway area of London, where my great-aunt Valentina liked to sit and 'wait out her exile', as she was wont to call her family's prudent decision to get out of Russia in 1919, when the civil war was just beginning. A time spent in Berlin culminated in the family wealth disappearing in the economic crisis of 1929. Valentina was packed off to London to safeguard any future, outside of poverty and dishonour, that she and her sister, Ariadna, might have expected.

During the war, she worked as a codes translator. With the descent of the Iron Curtain, Valentina gave up hope of returning to her beloved St Petersburg, as she still referred to it, even through its renaming, first to Petrograd, then Leningrad. "What will come next?" she used to ask, 'Robrograd,' 'Murdegrad' and later, 'Nikitograd' mockingly provided as alternatives.

Over the years she built up a rug and carpet business, earned a comfortable living and eventually sold her interest in it to her younger sister, my grandmother. Now, she spent her time showing visitors and tourists around the magnificent Orthodox church she was proud to have on her doorstep, meeting other émigrés from old Europe, reading books and Russian newspapers brought to her by her dutiful son, and watching the world from her private table – as she regarded it – at La Macarena.

This was a café with just a touch of old-world elegance about it. The coffee came to the table good and strong, in small, stylish pots. When she first patronised the place, these had been silver-plated, but as they began to disappear into customers' handbags the owner, Señor

Roderigo took them all out of service and replaced them. Naturally, he retained the one from which Valentina was always served.

Whenever ordering her chocolate, she was reminded of Florian's in Venice, which she had often visited, and pondered on the paradox that in Europe, the more impoverished the country, the better the coffee, chocolate and patisseries. Why, she wondered, did the English loathe food so much? Her experience had been of post-war London, when the Corner Houses declined, and any revival in the tradition of afternoon tea was still a long way off.

For her, La Macarena was an oasis in the gastronomic desert that existed between three and six-thirty. The *eclairs* and *milles feuilles* were of an acceptable standard, and most of all, she enjoyed the company of Señor Roderigo, himself an exile from Franco's Spain. When he wasn't too busy, he would come and sit with Valentina, and they'd play 'Ain't it Awful?' together, while they watched the Free West going to hell in a handcart before their weather-beaten eyes. Valentina would play the opening gambit:

"When I was young, there would have been none of these indecent displays of flirting in public. People would have been horse-whipped for what I see them get up to on the open street. Children with their skirts as high as their belts; vulgarity, without any trace of class or style. And don't they *ever* wash their hair?"

Señor Roderigo was concerned by the lack of respect in young people nowadays, which made him fear for the future. But what disturbed him the most was the dishonesty.

"Do you know for how many coffee spoons I am losing in this moments, Señora Valentina? Many, many; and others things also. There never was so bad times, Señora Valentina. Never."

These gentle moans were never directed at their host country; only at those bad habits that freedom tended to breed. They were always a preamble to the main menu: the need they had to resurrect the shared feeling of missing their homeland. Even after all this time, it was the unwilled nature of their departure that made the ache in their hearts an almost physical sensation, giving them no peace.

They were comfortable and safe in London; that was how they could afford the luxury of complaining so much. Yet inside was a need they were unable to satisfy. It is little wonder the authorities of oppressive regimes employ exile as a punishment. For the people of some cultures, especially those within a large land mass, to be denied entry and free passage to their country of origin was more than they could bear. There were suicides among the exiled, not as a consequence of ill-treatment from the host community, but as realisation sank in – deeper and with the force of the wound from a turned knife – that they would never be able to do what most of us take so much for granted: go home at the end of the day.

For Valentina, this ache had diminished with the years, but never disappeared. Through her interest in the big church, she had retained some values from her long-estranged past. Sometimes, she got to converse with one sad and lonely émigré or another in her mother-tongue. She remained alienated and forlorn, but determined and indomitable.

She first encountered Mrs Giannokopoulos one morning before her stint at the church began. Valentina loved the building. Its icons and frescoes reminded her of a culture torn down and defaced by the 'Moscow Barbarians', as she referred to the Soviet government. She found in the icon painters an ability to see Orthodoxy, indeed life itself, in the round, rather than in the strict, linear fashion of Baroque and pre-Baroque European religious work. In icon paintings, anything might happen; there were so many layers of meaning to catch and hold the eye.

Then, she adored the spaciousness of the place, recalling the Kazan, and St Isaac's cathedrals of her beloved Pitr. And most of all, at this time of the day, there was the immense silence in which she could lose herself and find help to soothe the feelings within.

Thus she was disconcerted to notice that someone else was already in the church when she entered. And as she made out the quiet but persistent crying, it allowed the haughty, superior-minded aspect of Valentina's character to will this weeping woman gone from her establishment. So preoccupied was she with her sadness, Mrs Giannokopoulos remained unaware of Valentina for quite a while. When she did notice her, Valentina's haughty manner dissuaded her from acknowledgement. This strange, very English stand-off continued until both remembered where they were and exchanged their religious greetings.

Eventually, Valentina discovered from another churchgoer that Mrs Giannokopoulos was a Greek from Cyprus, whose house and land had been expropriated during the Turkish invasion. Once Valentina had established her *bona fides* as a prospective member of the exiles club, she felt it appropriate, indeed a duty, to invite Mrs Giannokopoulos to sit with her at La Macarena.

"One mornin' I'm goin' about things ass usual, an' I can't believe what I'm seein'. There's some soldiers in the streets; Turk, ehh," she sort of spat the name out. "I'm not believin' it, y'know? In *my* village, *my* home. Turk! We stay away from them, but they come to our doors n' say we have to pack our things n' leave. Can you imagine this? Ah'm so angry, but also sad, 'cos it's come out of the blue, an' all the men are bin' taken away somewhere, with these Turk. So thassit; the British consul come and look at our papers, an' tell us we can go to Englan' if thass what we want, 'cos we got the family there, in London, in Wood Green Lanes. An' when we get there, what you thin' we find? Is *more* Turk, yeh. Livin' there in the same street. I tell Yannis an' Olympia, I no stay near them. They find me this place near the big church, and I stay here till I go home. Tha'ss it! I no live near no Turk, whatever!"

Mrs Giannokopoulos started to cry once more, and Valentina passed her a few tissues from her capacious handbag. Mr Lesniak, embarrassed, got up to use the toilet, while Señor Roderigo, mouthing sympathetic 'tut tuts', made coffee for them all. When Lesniak returned, they all sat for a while, sipping silently and reflecting on what had been taken away from them. It was time for one of their favourite comfort strategies.

Senor Roderigo began, "In the summertime, it was hot, like a *sartena*." He mimed a rapid sideways action of a frying-pan being moved while heated on a cooking-range. "*That* was summer; not like here, where the sun iss too 'fraid of the rain an' wind to shine at all. Too hot for working. All the men, they came to our home for *comida*, you know, to eat. My father "– here, he made the sign of the cross – "owned the *bodega*. Outside, I could hear only voices in the *habitaciones*, but could see nothing. It was very strange but so comforting also. This iss how I remember my home. The cool tiles on my feet in the hot time of the day, and quiet voices coming from nowhere."

Mr Lesniak, who had survived beatings, work camps and deportation, was briefer. Music was the love of his life

"For myself," he offered, "home is wherever I keep Strauss's 'Four Last Songs'."

This concision tended to irritate the more expansive, less musically inclined Valentina, who would raise her eyes at this offering, and look to those seated at the exiles' table for support in her disapproval. However, I should add that when it came, my great-aunt's contribution had about it a delicacy and poignancy which counterbalanced her more arrogant and intolerant side.

Looking at Mrs Giannokopoulos, who was still dabbing at her reddened, tear-stained eyes now and again with Valentina's scented tissues, she said, "Our house, the one where we lived – we owned several others – is on the Fontanka, in St Petersburg. I grew up there, and I can honestly say it was the love of my life. To leave was physical pain, my dear. On the last day, I asked my Mother for the apartment key.

"'Why do you want that? It won't open these doors ever again, you know.'

"But I insisted, and out of pity, I imagine, she gave it to me. The important thing, my dear Mrs Giannokopoulos, is always to leave the key somewhere safe."

Reaching into that bag of hers, she withdrew a brass door key, freshly polished, about five inches long, and in her outstretched palm she held it in front of them all.

"My home is right here. In the palm of my hand. I can see it, smell it, taste it, even. It is what those 'Moscow Barbarians' cannot ever steal from me. Here, it is safe. Even if I never go back, this says that I can."

Let us leave them there, shall we; this table of strangers drawn to one another because they cannot go to their homes, as can you and I.

My grandmother died, and three and a half years later so did Valentina. It happened around the time the Soviet Union was falling apart. What passed for democracy was being rescued by the appearance, atop an army tank in Moscow, of 'that drunken buffoon, Yeltsin,' as she referred to him. Great-aunt Valentina was hard to please when it came to Russian politicians.

She never got the opportunity to go back to St Petersburg. I undertook a pilgrimage on her behalf. It seemed altogether the right thing to do. I was the only surviving blood-relative, and Valentina had left me the key in her will.

One freezing, February morning, I located the site on the Fontanka where the sturdy apartment block still stood despite Red Guards, White

Guards, Terrors with their midnight raps on the door, Fascist bombs, and starvation, lurking the streets like a silent, voracious animal, awaiting history's next challenge in what remained of the Russian Century.

Inside, the current owner, Mrs Staravoitova was sympathetic. Over tea, I told her about my great-aunt, and she related how St Petersburgers were coming to terms with the economic necessities of the post-communist era. Then, carefully and with a touching respectfulness, Mrs Staravoitova's little grandson took Valentina's shiny, brass key and placed it upon the mantelpiece in the living room, back in its home once more.

ELLIE TILL

Ellie is a lifelong Bognor Regis resident who has always enjoyed writing. This is the first time she has had a short story published. She is the final member of Bognor Regis Write Club that you will meet in this book, and our final story.

The Frog King

BY ELLIE TILL

"Thanks Tommy, see you back in a little while, good lad." Mr Wilson says as always, patting me on the shoulder as I leave the shop with the bag of papers.

I swing the bag over my back and mount my trusty old bike, keen to get the route done quickly this morning, so I might be able to grab some breakfast before I go to school. Invariably I end up daydreaming and therefore too late, making my tummy rumble halfway through Maths, which is really embarrassing because I sit next to Katie Evans, and she always looks at me like I'm some kind of alien who's invaded Earth just to annoy her while she does algebra.

I like a good daydream – I let my mind wander as I cycle past all the houses and imagine who lives inside. That little cottage down the alley, for example, I like to think is home to an evil old witch who lures kids in with sweets. And that big fancy one on the end of the big road, that's where that famous footie player lives with his fit girlfriend.

I know it's not really, but it's fun to pretend, and my mum's always said I have a good imagination.

Just as I'm about to round the next corner, a large figure appears as if from nowhere right in front of me and I have to brake suddenly, causing the paper bag to flip round my side and open, spilling papers onto the wet road.

The figure, looming over me in a huge trench coat and a hat covering their entire face, seems unfazed by this. I scramble to pick up the papers, trying not to notice the wet ones as I cram them hastily into my bag.

"I'm really sorry, I didn't see you −" I start to explain to the mysterious trench-coated person. I can't be sure if it's a man or a woman; it's still dark this time of day, and their face is in shadow.

The person stares at me with bright, unblinking eyes just visible in the morning darkness. Out of nowhere, I suddenly feel very cold. They lean forward slightly and raise their finger into the air, almost like they're trying to work out what direction the wind is blowing from.

I'm starting to freak out a little bit now. I put my foot on the pedal, ready to take off. Just as I'm about to leave, the person suddenly shouts at the top of their lungs, "PEACE BE TO THE FROG KING!" and throws their arms wide.

I hear a strangled scream, which I realise has come from me, and pedal away as quick as I can, not looking back.

Once I've gone far enough that I think the person is out of sight, I slow and catch my breath against a low wall. I'd probably find it funny in a few hours, I think, but not right now, when I'm trying to concentrate on getting my heartbeat back to normal.

After a few minutes, I resume my normal route. I'm pretty sure they must have just been one of the local crazies − we do get a few around here. It'll be a funny story to tell Jack and Rob later at school.

So I pedal on, pretty relaxed again now. I see a small frog cross my path and swerve to avoid it, only realising afterwards the coincidence of the event. 'The Frog King,' I think to myself, chuckling.

Still laughing, I turn another corner and topple straight to the ground at what I see. In front of me is what can only be described as a Giant Frog. Easily as tall as my dad, although admittedly much greener and slimier, the frog looks solemnly down at me with its huge yellow eyes, its chin pulsing with the iconic 'Ribbit' noise.

I stare at it, dumbfounded. I notice it's got a golden crown atop its bulbous head. "The.... The Frog King?" I offer, doubtfully.

The Frog King nods. "It is I!" he booms, his voice deep and gravelly. "You have stumbled upon my lair."

I look around me, uncertain. His lair? This is just Ringwood Road...

Then I realise. What is usually a pretty mundane suburban street has somehow melted away, and turned into an immense forest.

Tall, gently swaying trees surround me and the frog. Toadstools are sprouting from the grass around us, and I can hear birds that don't sound like the wood pigeon most frequently heard around here.

Bike and paper bag forgotten, I gaze open-mouthed around me and up into the now barely visible sky, thanks to the dense trees. I'm so busy marvelling at this change of scenery that I almost forget about the giant frog.

He croaks, as if to attract my attention. "Bow to me." He commands.

I stumble to my feet and do as he says. I don't feel it's wise to argue.

"I shall let you pass," he begins, "if you solve my riddle."

I must still be asleep, I think. This has got to be some kind of mad dream. I should really stop eating cheese before bed.

I decide to play along and see where the dream takes me.

"Of course," I reply reverently. "Thank you."

The King ribbits a few more times and looks at me, unblinking.

He draws a great, shuddering breath, and calls out, "GATHER!"

At once, the leaves on the trees begin to rustle, and I feel the ground beneath me rumble. From behind the many trees and bushes, several animals appear: bunnies, tails twitching; snakes, slithering along the wet ground; countless bugs and butterflies, and, yes, that's definitely a unicorn, its glossy silver mane shining in the moonlight...

The party assembles around us, and I feel hundreds of pairs of eyes on me. It seems I've got an audience.

The King speaks, "How far can a fox run into a grove?"

I stare back, panicking. My eyes search around me for inspiration. I catch the eyes of several foxes. They all look back at me as if to say, 'We're not helping you out with this one.'

"Erm," I say timidly, "How long do I have to answer this?"

The King does not respond and continues to fix me with his unnerving, yellow stare. The animals are completely silent, waiting. I decide it's best to venture some kind of guess. I try to recall something, anything I might have learned about foxes at school. They're ... nocturnal? Females are vixens ... they like to go through the rubbish in my street sometimes ... They live in dens? Or is that badgers?

I consider I don't have much to lose, and try to look and sound confident as I straighten my back and state, loudly, and clearly: "The fox can run into a grove for as long as the moon is out."

"INCORRECT!" the King booms, making me jump and trip backwards over the handles of my bike, still on the ground behind me.

There's a flurry of tails, wings and flopping ears as the animals respond to this. If I didn't know better... yes, that unicorn is laughing at me. The foxes look downright insulted.

Before I can defend myself, or apologise, the King declares: "The answer is halfway. For then, he is running out of the grove."

This is completely weird, I think to myself. If this is a dream, how did my brain come up with this riddle? I've never heard it in my life!

"Be gone." The King declares with a royal wave of his webbed hand, and the next thing I know, the trees, the animals, the King have all disappeared and I'm left standing alone, on Ringwood Road, my bike on the floor beside me and the newspapers making their escape down the pavement.

Dazed, I sit there for a few minutes, trying to make sense of what just happened. My stomach lets out a tell-tale rumble and I check my watch. Brilliant, late again.

Dear Reader,

Thank you for picking up and hopefully reading all your way through to this point.

If you have enjoyed these stories, please could you leave us a review on Amazon, Goodreads, or any other book review website you use? Or drop us a line at bognorwriters@gmail.com. If you say something nice I will do my best to pass it on to the writers.

If we have inspired you to write your own stories, and wish to join a writers group, good luck and we look forward to reading your future successes.

Julia Macfarlane